THE ADVENTURES OF ULYSSES

Retold by Anna Claybourne

With an introduction by Anthony Marks

Illustrations by Jeff Anderson

First published in 2002 by Usborne Publishing Ltd,
Usborne House, 83-85 Saffron Hill,
London EC1N 8RT, England.
www.usborne.com

A catalogue record for this title is available from
the British Library.

ISBN 07460 5200 6

Printed in Great Britain

Edited by Felicity Brooks & Anthony Marks
Series editors: Jane Chisholm & Rosie Dickins
Designed by Brian Voakes
Series designer: Mary Cartwright
Cover design by Sarah Cronin
Cover image by Barry Jones

CONTENTS

About The Adventures of Ulysses

The Adventures of Ulysses is a modern retelling of a series of ancient stories, some of which may be as much as four thousand years old. They are about the homeward journey of the Greek hero Ulysses (also known as Odysseus) after the end of the Trojan War. The war took place in the 13th century BC between the Mycenaeans (rulers of Greece at that time) and the Trojans (inhabitants of the city of Troy). This book describes how Ulysses, one of the leaders of the Mycenaean army, returned to his home on the Greek island of Ithaca after his victory against the Trojans.

This type of story is known as a myth, from the Ancient Greek word *mythos*, which means "spoken words" or "speech". Myths were not written down, but were passed on by story-telling. Around 700BC, Greek writers like Homer and Hesiod began to collect, organize and retell myths. One of Homer's most famous works, a long poem called *The Iliad*, tells the story of the last year of the Trojan War; another, *The Odyssey*, is about his return to Ithaca.

But nobody is sure who Homer really was. Most experts now agree that he probably lived about 2,700 years ago, although no written records of his life survive from that time. Today, seven Greek cities claim to be his birthplace. He may have come from the island of Chios, or from a Greek colony called Ionia on the coast of Asia Minor. It is likely that he was a bard (professional poet) who recited or sang his poems – much as the blind bard Demodocus does in chapter three of this book. And like many bards before him, Homer did not write his poetry down – it was memorized and passed on from one generation to the next, and only written down many years later. This makes it difficult to trace the origin of his work; in fact, some experts even question whether *The Iliad* and *The Odyssey* are by the same person.

Whatever their sources, the stories are powerful tales of adventure. Though their roots are lost in history, they have links to real people, events and places. For example, in the 1870s the remains of Troy were discovered by the German archaeologist Heinrich Schliemann at a place called Hisarlik in Turkey. Other places mentioned in these tales are easily identified in modern Greece, so it is not difficult to plot the routes taken by Ulysses and his crew. Archaeological evidence tells us that the Greeks were great sailors, boat-builders and navigators, and it is likely that Homer based many of his stories on the tales of voyages made by sailors who explored the Mediterranean coast.

But myths have a complicated relationship with history. Because they are so old, it is unlikely that we will ever know how closely they reflect real historical events. Ancient storytellers did not always make the same distinction between fact and fiction that we do, and they often wove myth and reality together. For example, we do not know now whether Ulysses was a real person. It could be that Homer collected many adventure stories and attributed them to one hero. Some later Greek storytellers added an extra layer of myth – that Ulysses was Homer's grandfather.

Also, while myths were partly historical tales, they had other purposes. They were told for entertainment, so other storytellers may have added in extra episodes and adventures to make their versions more exciting. Myths also had a religious purpose: they described the lives and relationships of the Greek gods and goddesses. The ancient Greeks believed that their deities intervened directly in the lives of humans, and myths were a way of passing on religious beliefs. For example, Ulysses is prevented from reaching home for so long because he upsets the gods, particularly Poseidon.

Possibly the most important feature of myths is that they can be retold in many ways. In the same way as Homer passed on older tales by retelling them, so his versions have been retold by countless writers who have embellished and embroidered them for their own readers. However old they may be, the stories in *The Adventures of Ulysses* are full of ideas that we all understand – bravery, adventure and loyalty – which may be why we love to re-write and re-read them over and over again.

The Search

Sitting in the sun outside the palace, Telemachus sighed.

"If only..." he could be heard mumbling to himself. "If only he'd come back!"

On the grass in front of the palace, it looked as if some kind of celebration was going on. A crowd of young men were drinking, eating, and generally enjoying themselves. Only Telemachus was alone. He sat on the ground, his chin in his hand, as the shouting and laughter of the partygoers drifted across the palace grounds.

He watched miserably as Antinous and Eurymachus finished playing a board game, and Antinous, always a bad loser, tipped the board over in a rage and sent all the pieces scattering into the grass.

Then he spotted

Amphinomus directing some servants who were rolling a barrel of wine out of the palace storeroom. His father's wine. He felt furious. Everything – the wine, the food, even the game, belonged to his father, King Ulysses, and the young men of Ithaca hung around the palace, day after day, helping themselves to all of it. And there was absolutely nothing Telemachus could do to stop them.

Telemachus tried to imagine Ulysses marching into the palace grounds, taking out a huge sword, and chasing all the uninvited guests away. But it wasn't that easy to imagine. He hadn't seen his father since he was a baby, and he couldn't even remember what he looked like. It was nineteen years since Ulysses had left for Troy to fight in the war. Everyone else who had gone was either dead, or back home safely. But Ulysses and his men were still missing.

"If only he'd come back," sighed Telemachus again.

Suddenly, in the distance, he noticed a strange figure standing at the palace gates. He got up to welcome the visitor. Although he didn't like the uninvited guests eating him out of house and home, he knew that a stranger should always be offered hospitality.

The visitor was tall and handsome, with rather unusual, shining grey eyes.

"Welcome to our house, sir!" said Telemachus, taking the man's long spear and beautiful shield.

"Please come in and have something to eat."

He led the man into the hall and ordered a servant to prepare some food.

"So," began Telemachus, when his guest had eaten, "who are you, and what brings you to Ithaca? It's nice to have a visitor from foreign parts."

"My name is Mentes," began the stranger, "from Taphos. But never mind about that. Where's Ulysses? I was expecting to find him here."

Telemachus sat up straight, looking startled.

"Oh yes, I've heard he'll be home soon," said Mentes. "In fact, I assumed all those people out there had gathered to welcome him back."

"Just the opposite," said Telemachus wearily. "They all hope he's dead! They're my mother's suitors, you see – her admirers. They just hang around trying to impress her, hoping she'll give up on ever seeing my father again, and choose one of them as her new husband. Well, I suppose she is a good catch – whoever marries her will become the next King of Ithaca and get this palace and all my father's possessions."

Mentes opened his mouth to respond, but Telemachus was so pleased to have someone willing to listen to his complaints that he couldn't easily be stopped.

"They don't even behave like proper suitors," he moaned. "They spend most of the time making a nuisance of themselves and partying night and day at my father's expense. The stupid louts," he added.

"So why doesn't your mother choose one of them?" asked Mentes, finally.

Telemachus frowned, thinking about his mother, Penelope.

"She just can't seem to make up her mind," he shrugged. "One minute, she says, 'I'm not getting married again. I'm sure Ulysses will be back soon.' The next minute, it's 'Oh, I'm sure Ulysses is never coming back. I promise, as soon as I've finished this piece of weaving, I'll pick a new husband.'

"The trouble is," Telemachus went on, "she just can't give up hope that my father will come home. But deep down, she knows she'll have to do something soon. The suitors won't leave until she's made up her mind, and there's nothing I can do to get rid of them – there are just too many of them, and they wouldn't listen to me anyway. My mother doesn't know how to get them to leave either. I mean, she can't exactly throw them out herself, can she? And all the palace guards went off with my father to fight in the war. And anyway..."

Telemachus moved closer to Mentes and lowered his voice. "I think she secretly likes having them around, or she'd find a way to get them to leave."

"Well," said Mentes encouragingly, "you can be sure of one thing. The moment Ulysses comes back, he'll find a way to get rid of them!"

In one way, the stranger's words comforted Telemachus, but in another they made him feel even more downhearted. "But where is he?" he said. "If only he would come back. But he never does!"

"Listen, Telemachus," said Mentes, leaning forward conspiratorially, "I've got some advice for you. You're not a child any more, and it's time you did something. First, call a meeting and tell these people exactly what you think of them."

"I can't do that!" groaned Telemachus.

"Yes, you can, Telemachus. Take control! You should show them who's really in charge around here. And then," Mentes went on, "I think you should go on a little expedition. Visit King Nestor in Pylos, and then King Menelaus in Sparta. Ask them what's happened to your father. If you hear that he's dead, then come back and help arrange a wedding for your mother. But if not, you'll have to prepare yourself for a fight. Because when he does get home, you'll have to help him do something about this bunch of idiots!"

Telemachus was a little taken aback by this outburst. But he was even more surprised when Mentes, standing up and spreading his arms out like wings, shot up into the air and disappeared through a hole which had appeared in the roof.

At that moment, Telemachus knew the stranger had not been Mentes at all. The flashing grey eyes, the spear and shield — Telemachus realized he had been visited by none other than Athene, the goddess of wisdom.

He had better follow her advice.

"Gentlemen," shouted Telemachus above the noise. His mother's admirers had all assembled at the meeting place, as he had requested. All the old lords of Ithaca were there too. Many of them were the fathers of the young men who were staying at the palace.

"Silence!" yelled Telemachus, even more loudly.

The crowd fell quiet, and everyone turned to stare at Telemachus. The older men gazed at him in admiration. They could see that Telemachus had grown up to be almost as tall, strong and good-looking as his father.

Telemachus cleared his throat. "I've asked you here today," he said, in his most official-sounding voice, "to discuss a problem that's been bothering me recently."

He paused and looked around him at the sneering faces of the suitors.

"Or, should I say, two problems," he continued.

"First, as you know, my dear father Ulysses is still missing. And I'm sure most of you can remember what a kind and generous king he was."

A murmur of agreement passed among the older members of the audience.

"And secondly," said Telemachus, taking a deep breath, "you may have noticed that a mob of hangers-on has been pestering my mother, the queen. In fact, many of them are the sons of the noble lords who are here today. And I have to say that I think their conduct is disgraceful. They've invited themselves to stay at our palace, and are eating us out of house and home and drinking all our wine. It's high time they left me and my mother in peace. If they don't, it's not for me to say what terrible punishment the gods might inflict on them!"

With this Telemachus angrily threw his spear down on the ground.

At first, no one dared say anything. Then Antinous, who always behaved as if he was the leader of the suitors, stood up in a swaggering, casual way.

"Ooooh, Telemachus, you are in a bad mood!" he mocked. Several of the other suitors started sniggering. "So you think the way we are behaving is disgraceful, do you? What about your mother? She's the one who started all this. If she doesn't want to get married again, she should say so. But oh no, she leads us on, and makes us think she's going to choose one of us any minute, and then keeps us waiting around for a decision!" He put his hand on his hip, batted his eyelashes and imitated Penelope's voice:

" 'Oh, Antinous! Oh, Amphinomus! Oh, you're all so gorgeous, I just don't know which one of you to choose!' " The suitors roared with laughter.

"How dare you!" stormed Telemachus. "She's never said such a thing! How dare you mock my mother! She's got a difficult decision to make!"

"And I'll tell you another thing," sneered Antinous, "she's a crafty old thing too. Ages and ages ago, she said to us, 'Oh, when I've just finished this piece of weaving, I'll choose a husband.' So we waited, and waited. And after a few years we thought it couldn't possibly be taking that long. Then, do you know what happened?"

Pretending not to know, the suitors jeered and shouted, "No, tell us what happened!"

Telemachus scowled and turned red. He'd heard this story many times before.

"One of her servants told us what she was up to," snorted Antinous, "and we caught her at it. Unpicking the weaving! Every night, she undid what she'd done during the day, so it would never be finished."

The suitors laughed and jeered louder than ever.

"Well, we've been keeping an eye on her since we found out about her little trick. We've made her finish it. So it's time she kept her promise. And, Telemachus, if Ulysses is gone, I suppose you must be the man of the house! So tell your mother to choose a husband, and make sure you throw a good wedding party. After that, we'll leave you alone. And not before!"

Antinous performed an elaborate bow to the rowdy suitors, and sat down with a smug look on his face.

"Listen!" growled Telemachus furiously through gritted teeth, "I am going to Pylos and Sparta to look for my father. And when he comes back you'll be sorry. That's all I've got to say." He grabbed his spear from where it lay on the floor and marched out of the meeting place.

"Huh!" said Leocritus, a young suitor, as the assembly gradually broke up. "Even if Ulysses did come back, there are loads of us, and only one of him, so we'd kill him anyway!"

"And I don't think Telemachus is going anywhere," added Leodes. "He's too pathetic."

Mumbling in agreement, the suitors all went back to the palace to start the day's drinking.

That night, while the suitors lay around the palace, a dark ship pulled quietly out of the bay below the palace. On its deck stood Telemachus, watching as Ithaca disappeared into the night. Next to him stood the goddess Athene.

She had helped Telemachus prepare the ship, and found him twenty sailors to man the decks. Now she called up a great wind from the north. All night long, and into the next dawn, the ship cut its way through the black waves.

The next morning, the ship sailed into the wide, welcoming bay at Pylos. Leaving the men on board, Telemachus and Athene made their way up the sandy beach. Athene was now disguised as Mentor, one of Ulysses's friends from Ithaca. But, even with her help, Telemachus was a little nervous.

"What will I say to him?" he panicked. "A wise old king like Nestor – a friend of my father's." After his unpleasant experience in Ithaca, Telemachus wasn't feeling very confident.

They could see the king in the middle of a large crowd outside the palace. Some kind of sacrifice was obviously being made. Nestor, seeing them some way off, leaped up and began waving vigorously. Telemachus noticed that he was very old, with a jolly, round face, a tangled, grey beard and a small, golden crown. Now Nestor was urging the people around him to wave and beckon too.

"Visitors!" he cried, as Telemachus and Athene approached. "Excellent! And very well-timed – we're just about to start a feast to pay our respects to Poseidon. Come and sit down, the pair of you. Who are you, and where are you from?" He grasped Telemachus's hand and shook it warmly. "I must say, your face rings a bell. And you, sir." He now shook Athene's hand so hard that her shield slipped from her shoulder. She smiled.

"Your majesty, my name is Mentor," she began. "But this friend of mine is a much more important guest." She prodded Telemachus.

"Er... royal sir," stumbled Telemachus. "Your Majesty. We are from Ithaca, and I am Telemachus. I'm searching for news of my father. I think you fought with him at Troy."

"Ulysses!" cried Nestor delightedly. "Of course! I knew you reminded me of someone. Oh, my dear boy, you're very welcome. I remember it as if it were yesterday, fighting alongside your father on the fields of Troy. What a great man he was!"

"Was?" said Telemachus, hesitantly. "Please, your majesty – don't spare my feelings. Tell me – is my father dead?"

"Dead? Ulysses? Oh, no, no, no, I shouldn't think so," said Nestor. "A great fighter like him? The most cunning, brilliant strategist in the world?" Nestor sat down so heavily, that his old jowls wobbled.

"Well, actually, to tell you the truth, I don't really know," he said, rather more seriously. "The thing is, when we left Troy, we all got separated, you know. I eventually got home safely, and so did most of the others. Poor old Agamemnon, of course, when he got back, his wife had run off with Aegisthus. Then Aegisthus went and killed Agamemnon on his own doorstep. Tragic business. And his brother Menelaus wasn't there to protect him, as he'd been blown off course and ended up in Egypt. So as you can see, we were all over the place. Ulysses was blown off to the south somewhere, but that's the last I heard of him.

"But don't you worry, my boy. I'm sure Ulysses can get himself out of any scrape."

"We in Ithaca are desperate for him to come home," said Telemachus solemnly. "If only I were as great and clever as him, I might be able to get rid of the crowd of suitors that are plaguing my mother."

"Ah yes, I've heard about that." Nestor nodded. "You must get rid of them. You could do with a bit of help from Athene – I must say she hasn't been much use recently!" He roared with laughter, while Athene spluttered into her wine.

"Listen, my dear boy," Nestor continued, kindly, "I truly believe Ulysses is still alive. Here's what to do. Visit Menelaus. Oh, poor old Menelaus isn't much of a laugh these days, but he has been abroad a lot more recently than I have. He's the one who might know something about Ulysses and where he is."

The following evening, Telemachus found himself sitting in the huge, grand hall of King Menelaus in Sparta. Next to him was Peisistratus, one of Nestor's sons. Nestor had sent them there in a chariot, while Athene stayed with the ship. The two young men had received a solemn welcome into the echoing palace, where they were now being given supper. The King had not yet asked them who they were.

"Peisistratus," whispered Telemachus to his companion, "isn't this palace incredible? It's so huge and full of treasures. This must be what Zeus's palace looks like."

Menelaus heard him. He raised a sad, old eyebrow. His long, red hair, streaked with grey, hung down on either side of his long, weary face. "I don't think so," he said, coldly. "I can hardly compare myself with Zeus."

"Sorry," mumbled Telemachus.

"After all the hardships I've been through. Fighting a ten-year war to get my wife back from the Trojans. Being stuck abroad for eight years after that. Then coming home to find my brother Agamemnon dead. And losing my dear friend Ulysses."

"Ulysses?" said Telemachus, urgently. "That's what I..."

"Ulysses!" a woman's voice cried out behind them. "It can't be!" Menelaus's wife Helen had appeared in the doorway.

"What are you talking about, woman?" grumbled Menelaus.

"He looks just like him!" cried Helen. "For a moment I thought... But he must be Ulysses's son, Telemachus. Doesn't he look like him, dear?"

"Your Majesty," broke in Telemachus, "I am Ulysses's son, and I need to find out what happened to my father. Please, sir, tell me anything you know. Have you heard where he is? Is he alive or dead?"

"It happened in Egypt," began Menelaus slowly.

Trembling, Telemachus put down his fork. He was sure he was about to hear some terrible story about his father's death. Menelaus told them that when he was in Egypt, he had been stuck on an island called Pharos, waiting for the right wind to sail home. There he had met Eidothee, daughter of the god Proteus, the Old Man of the Sea. She had told him that her father would help Menelaus get home and answer any questions he had.

"I suppose that was very lucky," said Menelaus. "And when I asked Proteus how I could get home, do you know what he told me the problem was?"

Telemachus tried not to show his frustration at how long the king was taking to get to the point.

"He said we hadn't been making enough sacrifices," said Menelaus indignantly. "So all we had to do was make a sacrifice, pray to the gods, and we were on our way. It was that simple," he added, huffily.

"But... what about Ulysses?" asked Telemachus nervously.

"Ah yes. I was coming to that. Well, of course, I asked Proteus for news of all my friends, and he told me where Ulysses was."

"Yes... ?" said Telemachus.

"It's just a question of whether he can get back. That's the problem," mused Menelaus.

"So... where is he?" asked Telemachus, trying to hide his desperation.

"He's on an island," announced Menelaus. "Miles from anywhere. A nymph called Calypso is keeping him prisoner. According to Proteus, he sits on the beach, weeping for home, but Calypso won't let him go. Poor chap," added Menelaus, vaguely.

"He's alive," whispered Telemachus. "He's alive!" he shouted, hugging Peisistratus and laughing out loud. His voice echoed round the draughty hall. "Thank you, Menelaus! Come on, Peisistratus! I've got to get home!"

In the palace in Ithaca, a young merchant named Noemon stood before Antinous and the other suitors.

"I... I just came to find out if you knew where Telemachus was," he spluttered. "It's just that he's borrowed my ship to go to Pylos, and, well, I'll be needing it back soon."

"You lent Telemachus a ship?" shouted Antinous, standing up and knocking over several wine cups.

"Well... of course. He is the Prince of Ithaca. Er, why?" asked Noemon weakly.

"That sneaky, impudent little rat!" fumed Antinous. "That pathetic, stuck-up, useless little TOAD! He's gone off without telling us! Crept off in the night like a common thief! I'll show him. I'll teach him. I'll..."

"He did tell us, actually," put in Amphinomus. "At the assembly."

"Shut up, Amphinomus," Antinous snapped.

"I'm going to put a stop to that little idiot's plans once and for all. He's not going to get away with this. He's not going off to play the hero and find his father. Get me a ship! He'll come back past the islands at Asteris. Everybody does. That's where we'll catch him." Antinous's fist closed around the handle of his sword.

"And kill him!" he snarled.

Escape from Calypso

Dawn rose over Mount Olympus, bathing Zeus's palace in a pink, glowing light. The gods were sitting in a circle in the palace courtyard. Every morning, they assembled here to discuss what the humans were up to.

The gods fell silent as Zeus appeared with his long, white cloak brushing the ground and the shield he always carried sparkling in the sunlight. But Athene was so eager to start her story that Zeus had hardly sat down on his throne before she began.

"What's the point of being a good, kind and generous person," she shouted, making some of the gods jump, "if you end up miserable and lonely, stuck on an island miles from anywhere?" Everyone looked blank. They had no idea what she was talking about.

"Look at poor Ulysses," Athene went on. "He's been a wonderful king, ruled all the people of Ithaca as kindly as if they were his own children, and practically won the battle of Troy single-handed," – here Zeus raised his eyebrows just a fraction – "and instead of being allowed to go home to his wife, he's left to languish on the island of Ogygia. He's been there for seven whole years! That mad nymph Calypso has him in her clutches, and there's no way he can escape without our help."

Zeus, the great god of the sky, gave his daughter a weary smile. "Well," he sighed, sadly. "If people will mess with a Cyclops and upset my brother, what can they expect?"

Athene had to admit it was true. Ulysses had blinded the Cyclops – who just happened to be the son of Zeus's brother, the bad-tempered sea god Poseidon. From that day to this, Poseidon had done his utmost to stop Ulysses from getting home.

But Athene hated her uncle far more than she blamed Ulysses. "Ulysses had to do what he did to escape from the Cyclops," she said indignantly. "And Poseidon's nothing but a big old bully." Some of the gods looked around nervously. Then they remembered that Poseidon was away. He'd gone to Africa, where a huge sacrifice was being made for him.

"You're the leader of the gods!" pressed Athene. "You've got to do something while he's gone!"

Even as she spoke, Athene could see that Zeus had made up his mind.

"Hermes," he said loudly, turning to his son, the messenger of the gods. "The gods have decided that Ulysses has suffered enough. You are to go to Calypso immediately and tell her she must let him leave her island. He will have to make his own boat, and after twenty days at sea he will reach the land of the Phaeacians. They will help him return to Ithaca."

Zeus had spoken, and Hermes knew that Zeus must be obeyed. It was a long journey to Ogygia,

Calypso's island, and he really didn't feel like going, but he tried to look enthusiastic as he put on his winged sandals. Then, casting an irritated glance at his half-sister Athene, Hermes leaped into the air and flew up, up into the misty early morning sky, and headed in the direction of Ogygia.

As the sun began to sink in the west, Hermes touched down at last on the sandy beach, and walked wearily along the shore in the direction of the cavern where Calypso lived. A copse of fragrant cypress trees grew around it, and in their branches sat horned owls and flocks of black choughs, who filled the air with their chattering and chirruping. A vine, laden with large bunches of ripe grapes, twisted and tangled around the cavern's entrance, and four tiny, crystal-clear streams trickled across the sand past Hermes's feet. When he stepped closer, he could smell the heady scent of cedar and juniper logs burning inside the cave, and hear the nymph singing softly to herself.

Even Hermes, who lived in the gorgeous palace of Zeus, had to admit that Calypso's home was absolutely beautiful. He stood and gazed, enjoying the relaxing sounds and scents and the warm sun on his back. Finally, he stepped into the shady cavern.

"Calypso?" he ventured.

"Hermes, my dear!" cried Calypso. She leaped up from the loom where she'd been weaving, ran across the floor, and took Hermes by the shoulders, kissing him firmly on both cheeks. He blushed.

"What on earth brings you here? I haven't seen you in ages! And haven't you turned out well? The gods must have been thinking kindly of me, to send me such a handsome visitor! So, what can I do for you? But wait, don't answer any questions yet. The most important thing is that we get some food inside you."

"Oh," said Hermes. "I mean, thanks."

He hadn't expected to stay for dinner, but he realized he was feeling rather hungry after his long journey. Calypso was already putting a dish of ambrosia — the food that the gods loved best — and a drink of sweet nectar on a table for him. As his eyes got used to the gloom, he looked around the cavern at Calypso's beautiful woven wall hangings and precious ornaments.

But Ulysses was nowhere to be seen.

When he had eaten, Hermes knew it was time to answer Calypso's questions. It wasn't going to be easy.

"Calypso," he began. "The reason I'm here is... well... Zeus sent me. I wouldn't have come otherwise." Calypso looked slightly hurt.

"I mean," Hermes said quickly, "it was an awful journey – really boring! There wasn't even an island to have a rest on, and no one to offer me any sacrifices, and..." Calypso was staring at him. He'd better just say it. He took a deep breath. "I have a message for you," he said. "From Zeus. It's about Ulysses."

Calypso's face fell.

"Well, he has been here for seven years. And he really does want to get home to his wife. Zeus says you have to let him go."

Calypso was looking so heartbroken that Hermes didn't know what to do next. He knew she would have to obey Zeus. Everyone had to. So perhaps, Hermes thought, it would be better if he just left. "Calypso," he said. "I'm sorry..."

"This is absolutely typical of Zeus!" cried Calypso suddenly. Her miserable expression had changed into one of fury. "Those gods just can't let anyone have any fun. They're so jealous whenever a goddess wants to live with a mortal. I rescued Ulysses from the sea! I saved him, when the other gods would have let him die! And now they won't let me keep him! It's absolutely outrageous!" Calypso was standing up now, thumping one fist on the table, so that the plates rattled. Hermes could see she was close to tears.

"Well..." he said, nervously. "I'd better be going."

Calypso sat down heavily and covered her face with her hands. She said nothing.

"Thanks for the food," mumbled Hermes. He backed out of the cavern quietly, took off from the beach, and headed for home.

Calypso walked along the shore. She knew she would have to obey Zeus, however unhappy it made her. She approached the rock where, every day, her homesick captive sat gazing out to sea and weeping for his homeland. As she got nearer, she could make out his shape. His head hung forward. His feet dangled sadly over the water. His shoulders shook with wave after wave of deep, heavy sobs. She knew he wanted to go home, but she couldn't help wishing he would rather stay.

True, she had forced him to live with her like a husband for the past seven years. Every night, he came home to her cavern, and was as polite and kind as he could be. But, deep down, Calypso knew that however nice she was to him, whatever delicious food she cooked, and however often she washed his clothes and prepared hot, scented baths for him, she could never win his heart or make him happy. Every day, he sat on his rock, sobbing wretchedly. All he wanted was to leave.

"Ulysses," she said softly, touching his shoulder. He looked up at her. His usually beautiful face was wet with tears, his eyes were puffy, and his hair was bedraggled.

"Ulysses," Calypso repeated. "I've had a message from Zeus. There's no need for you to stay here any longer. You're free to go."

Ulysses had been so miserable for so long that at first he didn't believe her. He was convinced this must be a plot to keep him on the island forever.

He pushed his hair out of his eyes, wiped away his tears, and climbed off his rock.

"Calypso," he began. "How can I escape from this place, even if I am free to go? I have no boat or crew, and everyone knows that the seas around Ogygia are deadly. I'll just find myself washed up on your shores again. How can I be sure this isn't a trick?"

"Oh, Ulysses!" Calypso teased. "That just shows the crafty way your mind works, you wicked man! I promise you, Zeus has ordered me to let you go. I'll even help you build a ship. I swear I'll never try to harm you. How could I? It's not me that has been hard-hearted and unloving all these years! Not like some people."

And yet, back at the cavern, Calypso couldn't resist trying one last time to persuade Ulysses to stay. She looked at him with unblinking eyes.

"So," she said, "I expect you're overjoyed to be going back to that wife of yours."

"Calypso," began Ulysses. "I don't mean to be rude. I just..."

"But Ulysses..." She leaned nearer to him. "She can't really be better-looking than me, can she? I mean! A mortal woman, more attractive than a nymph?"

Ulysses had to think quickly. "My lady," he said politely, "of course, my wife's appearance could never compete with yours. She is a mere mortal, whereas you have perfect, unfading beauty. You are the most beautiful thing I have ever seen. Why, on that day, seven years ago, when you pulled me from the sea, I thought I must have been dreaming."

Calypso looked quite pleased.

"However," he went on, "it is my home, my kingdom, that I yearn for – to be among my own people, to feel the familiar soil of Ithaca beneath my feet, and to see my son, Telemachus, who I left behind when he was only a baby. He'll be a young man now."

Four days later, Ulysses's new ship bobbed proudly at its mooring, and Ulysses, wearing a set of new clothes that Calypso had given him, was itching to get going.

"So," he said, as brightly as possible, to Calypso. "This is it, then!"

Calypso didn't speak. She watched as he waded out to his boat, climbed on board and untied the mooring rope.

"Goodbye," he shouted, as a fresh wind, which Calypso had summoned up, nudged the boat away from the beach where she stood. "Goodbye, Calypso!"

Calypso watched until the ship was a small speck in the vast, shining ocean, and Ulysses was too tiny to see. Then she turned and walked back to her lonely cavern.

Ulysses couldn't remember when he had ever felt happier. The wind filled his sails, the sun was shining, and he was getting farther away from Ogygia by the minute. He was so excited, he couldn't even sleep. At night, he sat watching the stars, thinking of Ithaca. And even though the seas around Ogygia are famous for their dangerous currents, his boat sailed on safely for seventeen days, carried by the fair wind Calypso had summoned up.

On the morning of the eighteenth day, the sun rose on a beautiful sight. In front of him, rising up from the misty surface of the sea, was the mountainous land of the Phaeacians. Ulysses knew that these sea-loving people, who were close relations of the gods, would welcome him and help him on his way. As his ship sailed swiftly in to the land, Ulysses relaxed. He would soon be home.

"Curse him! Curse Ulysses! What on earth do those stupid gods think they're doing? I only have to go away for a few days and they go and change their minds without consulting me. Me, Poseidon, the mighty ruler of the waves! They'll regret this! Or at least," said Poseidon, remembering that Zeus, and not he, was ruler of the gods, "that puny little idiot Ulysses will regret it. He'll be sorry. There's no way he's getting back to Ithaca without a fight!"

Poseidon was on his way home from Africa. He was taking a rest at the top of the Solymi mountains when he had noticed the little ship. The last he'd heard, Ulysses was stuck on Ogygia, and that had suited the sea god very well. It served Ulysses right for injuring Poseidon's son. But now, he seemed to have escaped.

However, Poseidon still had the upper hand. Ulysses was out at sea, and that was the one place where the god could do his worst.

Poseidon grabbed his trident. "All right, Ulysses," he growled. "Now we'll see who's boss!"

Ulysses felt a cold wind on the back of his neck that made him shiver. He heard a very faint, low rumbling sound in the distance. He turned around.

Behind him, the sky was black. Thunder clouds were gathering on the horizon, and the wind whipped the waves up into frothy peaks.

Far away, below the darkest part of the sky, Ulysses could see a huge wave, the size of a massive cliff, rolling steadily closer. Meanwhile, the wind began to toss and buffet the ship so that Ulysses could hardly stand upright on the deck. He clung to the helm, wrestling with the current, while keeping a fearful eye on the menacing wall of water roaring in his direction. He wondered if these would be the last few moments of his life.

"I should never have expected to make it home safely," he moaned, "with my record of bad luck. My friends who died at Troy were the lucky ones – buried and celebrated as great heroes. I wish I'd died there too, instead of a lonely death here, in this cruel ocean!"

Ulysses was so wrapped up in this self-indulgent train of thought that he didn't realize the wave was almost on top of him. Suddenly it surged down with a huge, thundering roar, crashing all over the deck, whirling the boat around and snapping the mast in two like a matchstick. His hands were torn from the helm and he was flung off the deck.

He found himself deep underwater, dragged down by the weight of the clothes that Calypso had given him. The more he kicked and struggled, the heavier he seemed to become. His lungs were screaming for air, and when he opened his eyes, all he could see was a mass of swirling bubbles, filling his field of vision.

Finally, after fighting his way up until he thought his lungs would explode, he burst out on the surface of the sea, gasping desperately for air and coughing out bitter seawater. He was exhausted, but he thrashed through the waves to catch up with the boat, which was drifting, battered and broken, without its mast or sail. Hauling himself aboard, he collapsed onto the sodden deck.

And there he lay, almost comatose, clinging to a broken plank, while the winds threw the listing boat from side to side, and bolts of jagged lightning plunged into the sea around it.

"Ha!" barked Poseidon. "That'll teach him. Not so smug now, eh, Ulysses?"

He packed up his trident and went on his way, feeling satisfied with a job well done.

But someone else had been observing Poseidon's bullying. The goddess Ino, who was once human, but who now lived under the sea, was not so heartless.

"That poor Ulysses!" she said to herself. It almost made her cry to see how proudly and hopefully he had set out, and how near he had come to safety, only to have his boat smashed to pieces and his plans ruined. She decided to help him.

Ulysses groaned. He thought he must be hallucinating. Through the driving rain, he thought he could see a huge seagull perched on the ship's prow. He dragged himself closer. No, it was a woman – in a long, bluish-white dress. The rain and wind didn't seem to affect her. She wasn't even wet. Instead, a gentle glow hovered around her.

"Ino... ?" ventured Ulysses.

"Ulysses," Ino answered. She seemed to be fading in and out of sight, and her voice was as soft as the lapping of tiny waves on the shore. "I will help you – but you must follow my instructions.

"Your ship is bound for the deep," she went on, "and you will not reach land under sail. Swim, Ulysses. It's your only hope." She unwound a shimmering veil from her shoulders and held it out to him. "Tie this around your waist, and you may swim ashore safely. The veil will protect you. As long as you are wearing it you cannot drown or be killed, but the moment you reach the shore, you must cast it back into the sea and turn your eyes away at once."

She was gone. Ulysses was left half-sitting, half-lying on the deck, clutching the veil. It felt as soft as a seagull's feather.

He looked around. Maybe the storm was beginning to die down, but the land looked too far away to swim to. Perhaps, if the weather was improving, he could make it in his damaged ship, after all. He had not really listened to the goddess.

Yes, the storm was definitely subsiding. He hauled himself upright and took his place at the helm. A beam of sunlight peeked through the clouds.

"So," said Ulysses out loud, "even when the sea god does his worst, he can't hurt me. Can you, Poseidon?" he shouted rudely. "Eh? Ruler of the waves? I'm going to get home safe and sound, whatever the sea throws at me. Just you watch!"

Poseidon stopped dead in his tracks. Was that Ulysses he could hear, mocking him?

He turned slowly around.

"Ulysses," he roared. "Ulysses – you smug, arrogant, insignificant little FOOL!"

But all Ulysses heard was a sudden roar of wind, a huge thunder crash and the terrible sound of another giant wave, even bigger than the first, which smashed down all over his crippled boat. This time the ship splintered into thousands of pieces and Ulysses was plunged even deeper into the swirling sea. Kicking his way up to the surface, he fumbled with the silky veil and managed to tie it around his waist. When he finally emerged spluttering from the waves, there was nothing left of the ship at all.

For two whole days Ulysses was lost in the sea, sometimes drifting nearer to the land, sometimes being dragged helplessly away from it. Then, at last, the weather cleared, and he could swim closer to the Phaeacian coast.

But at first, he couldn't find a safe place to come ashore. The waves crashed onto the sharp rocks with such force that Ulysses was sure he'd be slashed and battered to death. "All my trouble has been for nothing," he complained to himself. "I'll end up breaking every bone in my body on those rocks. Or I'll get carried back out to sea, where I'll drown. Or I'll get eaten by a sea monster!"

He had forgotten that the magic veil would protect him.

Then a large wave threw him straight at one of the sharpest rocks of all. He saved himself from being smashed against the cliffs by grabbing the pointed tip of the rock with both hands, but the backwash dragged him off again, leaving several pieces of his skin clinging to the jagged stone.

Clenching his smarting fists, Ulysses felt like giving up. He was sure he would never see his home again. He could just let go, and sink down into the dark depths, let his lungs fill with salty water, let the current take him...

Through his half-closed eyes, he thought he saw a gap in the rocks. Slowly, he swam nearer to it, using the last few ounces of strength left in his body. It was the mouth of a stream, surrounded by grassy banks. He could feel the cool current against his aching legs, where the stream flowed fast and fresh into the sea. For the first time since leaving Ogygia, Ulysses remembered to pray for help.

"River god," he groaned faintly to the stream. "Please, please help me. Take pity on a poor sailor, and bring me ashore."

The stream's current slowed, then stopped, and the

sea became smooth and calm in front of him. He paddled up into the shallow, sandy mouth of the little river. There he fell on his knees, clumsily untied Ino's veil, and let it float back into the ocean, turning his face away.

The flesh on his arms and legs was all swollen. His cut hands throbbed, and salt water streamed from his nostrils and mouth.

He had to sleep. He stumbled onto the bank and crawled across the grass to a little grove of olive bushes near the rocks. Beneath their tightly-packed branches, where the thick growth of foliage let in no light, and fallen leaves covered the ground like a carpet, Ulysses lay down. His eyelids drooped drowsily and his heavy limbs sank into the soft leaf-litter. Finally, the goddess Athene sent Ulysses a deep, magical sleep, to renew and refresh him for the troubles that she knew lay ahead.

A Royal Welcome

"Nausicaa!" whispered a soft voice in Princess Nausicaa's ear.

"Nausicaa, what can you be thinking of? You haven't been there for ages!"

Nausicaa was having a very confusing dream. In the dream, her best friend, Eugenie, was talking to her. Nausicaa rolled over sleepily under the precious eiderdown, embroidered with golden thread, that covered her bed.

"Haven't been where?" she murmured in her sleep.

"To the river, to do your washing, of course!" said Eugenie. "Just in case!"

Eugenie started giggling.

"In case what?" Nausicaa didn't understand. She was a princess. She didn't have to do the washing.

"In case you get married," laughed Eugenie. This dream certainly was very odd. "It's important for a girl to do a lot of washing," Eugenie went on. "It's good for your reputation and gets you on the right side of your parents. Because all the men in town have their eye on you, Nausicaa. I mean, you're the princess of Phaeacia! They're all going to start asking to marry you any minute. And you'll need lots of clean clothes. I'm telling you, you'd better go to the river tomorrow."

What Nausicaa didn't realize was that the goddess Athene had come into her dream, disguised as Eugenie, and whispered to her as she slept. Athene wanted Nausicaa to go the river so that she would find Ulysses, who was asleep under the olive bush, near the mouth of the river.

And when Nausicaa woke up, she somehow did want to go to the river. It was true, she hadn't been there for ages. She could go with her maids and have a day out.

"Father," began Nausicaa carefully. She couldn't say she wanted to go to the river to prepare for getting married – that would be far too embarrassing.

"Do you think you could ask the servants to prepare a cart and mules to take me to do some washing at the river? There are loads of dirty clothes lying around, and you need clean things to wear for meetings, and my brothers need them for parties."

"Absolutely," said King Alcinous, without asking any questions. He knew as well as Nausicaa did that the servants could do all the washing. But he liked to indulge his only daughter. He let her do whatever she wanted.

Soon the wooden cart containing Nausicaa and her maids trundled to a halt next to the river, where a series of crystal-clear pools led down to the sea. The girls untied the mules and let them wander free to graze on the grassy banks.

It didn't take them long to wash the bundle of clothes which Nausicaa had managed to find. They rinsed them quickly, swishing them around in the swirling water, and laid them out along the banks to dry in the warm morning sunshine. Then it was time to have some fun. They bathed in the sparkling river, laughing and screaming as they splashed each other with droplets of water.

Ulysses, still in a deep sleep under the olive bush nearby, began to stir.

After their swim, Nausicaa and her maids sat on the bank in a group and rubbed each other with perfumed oil to keep their skin soft. Giggling, they combed their hair and tried on each other's clothes.

Ulysses thought he was having a dream about twittering sparrows.

When the hot sun was high overhead, Nausicaa's maids went to the cart and got the food they had brought. They sat feasting on the fresh fruit and cheese that the kitchen servants had packed for them, and made a small driftwood fire and toasted pieces of bread on sticks.

Ulysses started to dream of hot roast dinners. He turned over in his sleep.

At last, when they had finished eating, the girls took a ball from the cart and began throwing it around. Their laughter grew louder as they ran to and fro, flinging the ball higher and higher.

At that moment, the goddess Athene made the ball veer off to one side after a particularly forceful throw. It ended up in the river, where it started bobbing steadily down to the sea.

The girls shrieked.

Ulysses woke up with a start.

He sat up, brushing dry leaves from his legs, and remembered where he was. But what was going on? Who was screaming and making such a racket? He decided to go and find out. He got up, crawled out of the bush, and stumbled over to the river.

He saw a crowd of girls leaning over a particularly deep pool, trying to reach a ball with a stick. Nearer to him were the leftovers of their picnic.

Ulysses remembered that he hadn't eaten for days. He was about to call to them when he realized that he had lost most of his clothes in the sea. But he was so hungry, he would have to ask for help. He quickly tore a branch from the bush and held it in front of him.

"Er... hello!" he called.

This time the girls screamed louder than ever. Half-naked, encrusted in salt from the sea, covered in scabs and dirty dead leaves, with matted hair and filthy skin, Ulysses looked more like a mad wild animal than a man. Only Nausicaa stayed where she was, while her maids ran away over the grass and sand down to the sea.

Ulysses stared at the girl in front of him. She was incredibly beautiful.

"Lady, I must beg you to help me," he began, politely. "If you are a lady, and not a goddess. For I have never seen any human as beautiful as you. Your parents must be proud of you, and as for your husband, well, he'll be a lucky man.

"But I'm not so lucky. I've been at sea for nineteen days, and away from home for nineteen years, and now I find myself in yet another strange land. Please would you be so kind as to direct me to the nearest town, and to give me some kind of rag or blanket to wrap around myself?"

Nausicaa stared back at him. Then she remembered that, as princess of the country, she ought to welcome him.

"Sir," she said, "your politeness shows that you are a wise and well-bred man. I'm afraid your bad luck is the work of the gods, but while you're here in

Phaeacia, we'll do what we can to help." She stepped closer to him. "I am Nausicaa, the daughter of Alcinous, King of the Phaeacians," she added. Then she quickly called to her maids to bring the stranger something to eat.

When Ulysses had eaten what remained of the picnic, and bathed himself in the river, Nausicaa brought him a newly-washed, dry tunic to wear. She was amazed at how different he looked. Now that he was clean, he suddenly seemed very handsome, with thick black hair and strong, muscular arms and legs.

"Sir," said Nausicaa, "it's time for us to go back to the city. I'd like to welcome you to my father's palace, but the people would gossip if they saw me riding into town with a strange man. So when we reach the outskirts of the city, please wait in the forest outside the walls until our cart has gone in. Then follow us, and make your way to the palace.

"Walk through the great hall until you find Arete, my mother. She will be sitting by the hearth, weaving a beautiful tapestry with purple thread. Beg her to help you. If you can win her sympathy, I'm sure you'll be able to get home to your own land."

After waiting as Nausicaa had instructed, Ulysses walked through the grand gates of the Phaeacians' city. It was a beautiful place. Hundreds of white houses with blue-tiled roofs clustered around the port, where several tall, well-built ships were moored. In the distance, the blue-green sea shone in the sunlight.

There was no mistaking Alcinous's palace. It towered above the other houses, and was built of stone so white that it seemed to glow like the sun. It was surrounded by a gleaming wall of bronze, and a garden bursting with ripe pears, figs and grapes. Even though Ulysses was a king himself, he felt a little nervous about going in.

The goddess Athene helped him by shrouding him in a thick mist, so that no one could see him or challenge him as he strode through the great hall. At the far end, flanked by guards and noblemen, he could see Queen Arete, weaving her tapestry, just as Nausicaa had described. Although her face showed the wisdom of many years, she was still beautiful, and Ulysses could see that she resembled her daughter. Nearby sat her husband, Alcinous, a king renowned for his kindness and generosity. Ulysses prayed that they would help him.

The onlookers gazed in wonder at the strange patch of mist floating through the hall, but when Ulysses reached the royal couple, Athene made it disappear. Ulysses fell to his knees in front of the astounded queen, and began his speech.

"Queen Arete," he said. "May the gods grant you happiness. I beg you to help me return to my own land, for I have suffered many hardships since I last saw my friends and family."

There was a shocked silence. Everyone stared at the stranger who had suddenly appeared among them. Then Echeneus, an old lord, said, "Alcinous, it seems you have a guest. Surely we should welcome him."

The king stood up, took Ulysses by the hand, smiled warmly at him and led him to a seat.

"My lords," King Alcinous announced to the assembled noblemen.

"It is time for you to make your way to your own homes. Tomorrow, when you have reassembled, we

shall hold a general meeting, and arrange for our noble guest to be transported safely to his home."

Ulysses relaxed. Relief flooded through him. Perhaps, at last, his journey would soon be over.

Everyone was filled with excitement about the new stranger in town. This was partly because Athene had disguised herself as one of the king's messengers, and had gone around announcing that an amazing foreigner, who looked more like a god than a man, would be at the meeting place that morning.

She also used her power to change Ulysses's looks just a little. She made him taller and stronger, with thicker hair and an even more handsome face than he already had. Soon the meeting place was filled with an eager, gossiping crowd of people, all trying to get a good look at the newcomer.

"People of Phaeacia!" shouted King Alcinous above the din. The crowd quietened down.

"This noble stranger has asked us to help him reach his home. As it is the Phaeacian custom to help all seafaring visitors, let us prepare a ship, and pick fifty-two of our strongest young oarsmen to take him to his destination. Although," he added, looking at Ulysses, "He's so strong and handsome that, if he were willing to stay, I wouldn't mind having him for a son-in-law."

The crowd laughed and cheered, and young men began pushing forward excitedly to offer themselves as oarsmen.

"When the ship is ready, the crew and all my noblemen will be invited to a feast at my palace, to entertain our visitor before he leaves."

An even bigger cheer went up as the townspeople started hurrying down to the sea to prepare the ship. While the men were being chosen and the boat was being loaded with food and water, Alcinous ordered his servants to get the feast ready. He also called for Demodocus, the royal bard. He would sing songs of gods and great heroes to entertain the guests during the party.

A few hours later, the palace's great hall echoed to the sound of laughter and conversation. Empty bowls littered the tables. Servants walked from place to place, refilling the silver cups with water and expensive wine. The guests leaned back in their chairs, feeling relaxed, contented and full of the best food that Phaeacia had to offer.

"So," said Alcinous, banging the table, "if everyone has feasted enough, I think it's time for a song!"

The guests watched as Demodocus, clutching his silver harp, was led in by a servant. For although the bard had the most beautiful singing voice in Phaeacia, he could not see. Some said the gods had taken his sight away in exchange for his amazing talent.

Demodocus raised his harp and plucked a single note. An expectant hush fell over the hall and then the bard began to sing softly:

"My royal king, my fair and lovely queen,
I'll sing a tale that's known around the world,
About the hero Ulysses at Troy –
How Ulysses and brave Achilles fought,
And Agamemnon's heart was filled with joy."

Ulysses's stomach turned over when he heard what the song was going to be about. The Phaeacians didn't know who he was, but the story of the Trojan War had obviously spread far and wide while he'd been stuck on Calypso's island.

As the bard began singing, Ulysses was reminded of what had happened at Troy...

Achilles and Ulysses had both been on the Greek side in the war against the Trojans, along with

Agamemnon, Menelaus and the others. But they had fallen out at a banquet. Although the violent argument had shocked the others, Agamemnon had been secretly pleased.

Many years earlier, he had heard a prophecy from Zeus, which had predicted that when Ulysses and Achilles argued, the Greeks would win the war soon after. And win they had, but both Achilles and Agamemnon had been killed. And now, in the palace of the Phaeacians, as the bard sang about the brave heroes of the Trojan War, the beautiful sounds of the music made Ulysses weep for the friends he had lost.

Fortunately, he was wearing a heavy purple cloak, given to him by the king and queen. He used part of it to cover his face, so that the other guests wouldn't see him crying. He tried desperately to stop, reminding himself how bravely he had fought at Troy, but that only made it worse.

The longer Demodocus's song went on, the more Ulysses wept, until at last his shoulders could be seen shaking with sobs. King Alcinous couldn't help noticing, and several of the guests were beginning to stare at Ulysses.

The king motioned to Demodocus to stop singing. "I'm afraid our entertainment isn't to everybody's liking," he said kindly. "My friend, what is upsetting you? You've been weeping bitterly ever since the bard started to sing, even though this banquet and this entertainment were meant to please you."

Everyone peered at Ulysses. Some people nudged each other as he lowered the purple cloak, revealing his tearstained face.

"My friend," King Alcinous went on, "I beg you, please tell us who you are, and why you cry when you hear a song about brave heroes, when you should rejoice. Where did you come from, and what have you seen on your travels? You know, talking about your troubles can help to soothe them. Come, sir. Tell us your story."

He reached out and placed a hand warmly on Ulysses's shoulder. Ulysses wiped his eyes and took a deep breath.

"You are very kind, your majesty," he began, "and honestly, your bard is the best I've ever heard. There's nothing at all wrong with his performance. It's because of my memories that I got so upset. And since you ask, I will tell you who I am."

Only the clatter of a cup being put down broke the heavy silence. Everyone was agog with anticipation.

"I am..." Ulysses faltered. "I am the famous Ulysses, of whom your bard sings. The whole world speaks of my skill and bravery, yet no one but the gods knows where I have been, and how I have failed so miserably to reach my home again. This is my story..."

The Cyclops

"It's a sad tale," Ulysses began. "I set off from Troy in triumph, with twelve great ships laden with treasures, and I had a fine crew of men.

"Yet when I crawled onto your shores two days ago, I was destitute and alone. When you hear of the terrible monsters we met, you'll be amazed that anyone got out of it alive. But I have to admit," Ulysses added, "it was partly my own pride that caused our problems. If only I hadn't taunted the Cyclops..."

"You've had dealings with a Cyclops?" gasped King Alcinous. An excited murmur passed around the guests in the hall.

"Sorry," said Alcinous. "Do carry on."

"When the Greeks left Troy, our fleet split up. Agamemnon and Menelaus went off with their ships, and I thought we'd have no problem making our own way back to Ithaca. Instead, my convoy was blown off course in a huge storm sent by Zeus. We stayed awake for two days and two nights, trying to control the ships as they were tossed, battered and driven sideways by the gale. But we couldn't fight the wind. It blew us south, away from Ithaca and past the island of Cythera, into the open sea.

"We sailed for nine whole days with no sight of land, and we needed fresh water," said Ulysses, "so we pulled up at the first place we came to.

"It was the land of the Lotus-eaters. You'd think we would have been delighted to be met by a friendly race of people. But their friendship was dangerous.

"As soon as we'd found some water and had some dinner, a few of my men went to find out what sort of people lived there. As it turned out, the natives had no intention of attacking us, or even defending their own possessions.

"Oh no, they were only too willing to share what they had. The next thing I knew, my men were stumbling out of the woods with huge grins on their faces, and the juice of a sticky fruit running down their chins.

" 'We want to stay here forever,' they cried, like innocent children at a party. They had been given the fruit of the Lotus plant. Like a drug, it had made them forget that they had jobs to do, or even that they had homes to go to. They wanted nothing more than to spend their entire lives lazing around, eating Lotus fruit and forgetting all their troubles.

"Well, I wasn't falling for it. I personally dragged each man back on board and chained him up in the galley. Then the rest of the crew rowed us away from that place forever.

"After that, as you can imagine, we were wary of landing anywhere else, but we still needed a rest. And the next place we came to was the home of the Cyclopes. Of course, I'd heard all the stories – that the Cyclopes were a savage people, uncivilized and stupid, and that they could be dangerous. But I thought it couldn't be any worse than the land of the Lotus-eaters. I was wrong."

"We landed on a little offshore island. From there we looked across to the mainland, where we could see wisps of smoke rising through the trees. And we could hear these strange, booming voices. I was curious. I wanted to meet these people and find out just what they were like.

"So the next morning, I told the rest of the men to wait for us while I took my own ship and crew over to the mainland. And there, right by the shore, was a cave. Someone had built a thick wall of stones around the entrance, making a kind of yard. I decided this was the place to land, and I picked twelve men to go ashore with me. I also took along a little something – a goatskin full of strong wine. I planned to have it handy to give as a gift, in case we needed to get on the right side of anyone.

"The owner wasn't at home, so we tiptoed into the cave to explore. Inside, it was absolutely enormous. There were pens filled with bleating lambs along one side, and all the Cyclops's possessions were lying around – tools, baskets, huge pails of milk, and a pile of massive cheeses.

"By the size of those cheeses, we could tell this Cyclops was a particularly large giant. My men didn't want to hang around. They were all for trying to roll one of the cheeses down to the boat and getting out of there. And that would have been by far the best thing to do," said Ulysses miserably.

"But no, of course, I insisted on waiting until our friend the Cyclops came home.

"We were still debating what to do when we heard his footsteps outside. To be honest, they sounded more like thunderbolts. The next thing we knew, a huge pile of firewood – whole trees and branches – crashed onto the floor just inside the doorway, and we had to run for our lives. We scuttled to the back of the cave and hid there.

"Then, at last, we saw him towering in the cave entrance. He was vast. He looked more like a mountain than a person. His dirty, sticking-up hair looked like the trees on top of a mountain. And, right in the middle of his forehead, staring wildly from side to side, was the huge, single eye that all Cyclopes have."

All the guests in the hall drew in their breath in horror. King Alcinous looked pale.

"Of course, I'd heard that the Cyclopes were ugly, one-eyed monsters," said Ulysses, "but until you see that single eye," – he looked around the hall, from one wide-eyed guest to another – "until you actually see it, you don't realize just how horrible it is.

"Anyway," Ulysses went on, "by then, it was too late to escape. The next thing the Cyclops did was to lift up a massive stone slab and prop it across the entrance of the cave. It was bigger than anything we could lift. You couldn't even move it if you had twenty horses to help you pull. That's how big it was. All we could do was sit there and hope he was in a good mood. That's when he spotted us.

" 'Strangers!' the Cyclops bellowed in a voice so deep and booming that we felt the vibrations through the rocky floor. 'Strangers! In my cave?'

"We all huddled back against the wall, trembling. 'And who might you be, strangers?' he roared.

"I was terrified, but I put on my nicest, most charming voice. 'Greetings to you, sir!' I said. 'We are Greeks, on our way back from the battle of Troy, to our home in Ithaca. Of course,' I added, trying to sound light-hearted, 'we didn't mean to come here, but we got a little, er, blown off course. And if you would be so kind, sir, in the name of the almighty Zeus, could we beg you to help us on our way? Or might you perhaps entertain us in your beautiful home? Please?'

"He looked slightly puzzled for a moment. Then a frown passed over his stupid face.

" 'Hah!' he boomed. 'Zeus! In the name of Zeus! We Cyclopes don't give a fig for the name of Zeus! You must be an idiot if you think I'd help you for fear of him! But tell me,' he said, suddenly sounding more friendly, 'where's your ship, then? Eh? Is it somewhere up the coast? I'd quite like to see it.'

"I didn't trust him, so I had to think quickly.

" 'Er... our ship,' I said, 'yes, it's, er, shipwrecked. But we managed to escape. That's why we need your help. If you wouldn't mind.'

"In reply, the monstrous creature reached out his huge, hairy hand, and, before we could hide, grabbed two of my men around the legs, gripping them both in his fist. Then he lifted them up and smashed their heads against the stony floor, killing them instantly. Their skulls split open and their brains spilled out onto the ground.

"We could only watch in horror, rooted to the spot by fear and disgust, as he proceeded to tear them up, limb by limb, and eat every scrap of them — their skin and bones, even their clothes.

Some of the men started to weep as the Cyclops crunched on their comrades' bodies, and licked his bloodstained lips."

King Alcinous's hand was over his mouth. He didn't look well.

"Then," said Ulysses, "he washed it all down with an enormous slurp of milk, and lay down to sleep.

"You can imagine what was going through my mind. My heart ached, as I had lost two of my friends, and I was full of fury and hate for the Cyclops. And I felt bad for insisting that we stayed in the cave, when we could have left so easily before he arrived. I wanted to protect the remaining men from the monster. I took out my sword, planning to stab the Cyclops in the side and kill him. But I stopped myself just in time. If he was dead, we'd never escape – we'd be trapped forever by the huge stone slab over the cave door. I had to think of another plan.

"The next morning, exactly the same thing happened. The Cyclops got up, milked his ewes, and then grabbed two more of my men for breakfast. We couldn't bear to look. We turned away in agony as we heard their heads being cracked open and their bodies being chewed and swallowed. Then the Cyclops opened up the doorway, drove his animals out, and replaced the stone slab.

"All morning, I racked my brains. I had to think of something. I, Ulysses, whose strategies had helped to win the Trojan War! Surely I could get us out of this.

"It was a pole lying on the floor that gave me inspiration. It was probably just the Cyclops's walking stick, but to us it seemed as big as a ship's mast. We couldn't possibly lift it. So we hacked away at it with our swords and cut off a piece about the height of a man. I sharpened the end into a point, and hardened the point in the fire. Then we hid our new weapon under piles of smelly sheep's dung.

"The Cyclops only had one eye. And I only had one job in mind for that pointed stake."

"In came the Cyclops that evening, being careful to replace the slab behind him, and went through his ritual. He milked his ewes. He grabbed two of my terrified men, and killed them mercilessly. Then he gobbled them up in front of us.

"This was my chance. I took my goatskin of strong, rich wine and poured some into a bowl. I walked up to him, and tapped him on the foot.

" 'Here, Cyclops,' I said, in a sweet, coaxing voice. 'Please taste some of this delicious wine, which I brought especially for you. It will help you wash down that meal of tasty human flesh, which I can see you've enjoyed.'

" 'Shut up, stranger', thundered the Cyclops, grabbing the bowl from me. He tipped his head back and drained it immediately.

" 'MMMmmm!' he boomed. 'Delicious. Well, stranger, perhaps I've changed my mind about you. Be good enough to pour me some more wine, and tell me your name, so that I can give you a special present.'

"I poured him three more bowls of wine, and although it didn't seem very much for someone his size, it was so strong that it soon started to have an effect. His movements began to get clumsy, his speech was slurred, and he became more stupid than ever.

" 'So, sshtranger,' he drawled, 'what'sh your name, then. Uh? Are you going to tell me, or what? Uh?'

"I could hardly keep myself from grinning at my clever plan.

" 'Nobody', I told him. 'My name is Nobody.'

" 'Well, Nobody,' slurred the Cyclops, smirking stupidly. 'I'll tell you what your preshent will be.' Then he started laughing a horrible, gurgling laugh, and said: 'I'll eat you lasht. Out of all your comrades, I'll save you,' he guffawed, 'and eat you at the end. For dessert.'

"And then," Ulysses told the spellbound guests in the hall, "he fell over, with a thundering crash, and lay unconscious on the floor. He was flat on his back, snoring, with his head twisted over to one side. Perfect."

"We put the point of the wooden stake in the fire again to heat it up. Then my closest comrade, Eurylochus, and three of my other men lifted it up and carried it over to the sleeping giant. Meanwhile, he had vomited in his sleep, and a stinking stream of wine and chunks of human flesh had poured down his cheek.

"While I leaned on the end of the pole, my four friends twisted it, and together we drove it right into the middle of his huge, round eyeball. The blood welled up, boiling and sizzling around the burning hot wood. Foul-smelling smoke filled the air, and the heat singed the monster's big, bushy eyebrow. We kept gouging and twisting until we had dug out the very roots of his horrible eye.

"Pretty soon he woke up and started struggling and thrashing about. He let out a huge, blood-curdling scream that echoed around the walls of the cave, and sat up, shaking us off him like breadcrumbs. He put his hands up to his face, grabbed the stake and yanked it out of his eye, which just made the blood flow even more quickly. It poured down his face and neck as he clutched in agony at the ragged, smoking eye-socket."

"My goodness," said King Alcinous, weakly. His face had turned a delicate shade of green. Everyone else leaned forward, pressing closer around Ulysses. "What happened then?" asked Demodocus, the blind bard.

"Then," said Ulysses, "the second part of my cunning plan came into operation. The monster got up on his feet, and stumbled around the cave, tripping over milk pails and banging into the walls, and yelling 'Help! Oh, my friends, I am hurt! Help me!' And all the other giants came running from their homes, and shouted from outside the cave: 'What, Polyphemus? What's the problem? Who has hurt you?'

" 'Nobody!' bellowed the monstrous Cyclops. 'Nobody has hurt me! Nobody has blinded me!'

" 'Well then,' shouted the others, sounding irritated, 'what did you wake us up for?' And off they went, while I laughed to myself about how well my plan was working.

"But we still had to get out of the cave. In the morning, after groaning loudly all night, the Cyclops felt for the stone slab, and managed to heave it out of the way. Then he slumped down heavily in the cave entrance, and began to feel each animal as it passed by, so we couldn't sneak out. But I had another idea.

"In the flock, there were lots of large, woolly rams. I tied them together in threes, using some of the Cyclops's own yarn, and tied one of my men under the middle sheep of each group. That way, when the rams wandered outside, we would go with them. Because, you see, the Cyclops only thought to feel the back of each sheep, not the underside.

"For myself, I picked the biggest, woolliest ram of all. I clung onto his shaggy belly, and hung there upside-down as we waited for the animals to leave the cave."

"My ram, laden down with my weight, was the last to go. And as the giant stroked his back, with me clinging on for dear life underneath and hardly daring to breathe, I realized that even the Cyclops had a kind word for someone. One of his sheep.

" 'Dear, sweet ram,' he burbled, 'you're usually the first of the flock to trot outside in the morning, and the first to get to the lush meadows. Why are you so slow today? I expect it's because you're feeling sorry for me! You're depressed, aren't you, because your dear master has been blinded by that evil Nobody? Oh, if only you could speak, and tell me where he's hiding! I'd bash his brains out!'

"When I heard that, I clung on tighter than ever."

"Outside, I let go of the ram and untied my friends, and we ran down to our ship, boarded it, and rowed for the island as quickly as possible. But as soon as we were clear of the shore, I couldn't resist shouting: 'So, Cyclops, you've got your just deserts, now, haven't you? Zeus has punished you, as he should, for being so rude as to eat your own guests!'

"This infuriated him so much that he reached out and snapped off the top of a pinnacle of rock, and hurled it after us into the sea. It landed in front of us, sending up a huge wave that washed the boat back almost to the Cyclopes' shore. But I managed to push us away again with a long boathook.

" 'Ulysses,' groaned Eurylochus, 'please don't make him any angrier! Let's just get out of here as fast as possible!'

"But I was delirious with my success, and I couldn't stop myself.

" 'Cyclops!' I boasted loudly, 'if anyone wants to know who blinded you, tell them it was Ulysses of Ithaca, son of Laertes!'

" 'Ulysses!' growled the monster furiously. 'I'll make you pay for this!'

"Then he drew himself up to an enormous height, so that his cold shadow fell right across our ship, and threw his great arms up to the sky.

" 'Beloved father Poseidon, god of the sea.' he roared, 'I pray to you, and you alone. Ensure that Ulysses never gets home! Or if he does, let him arrive late, after years of misery, on an unknown ship, with all his comrades dead, and trouble brewing in his royal house!'

"And that is why," concluded Ulysses, "the mighty Poseidon has cursed me throughout my journey, and sends me storms wherever I go. If only I had listened to my men, and held my tongue," he said sadly, "I might already be home. In fact, soon after we left the land of the Cyclopes, we came so close to Ithaca that we could see the people waving on the shore, and I was sure I was about to see my family and friends once again. And yet it was not to be.

"But that," said Ulysses, reaching for his wine, "is another story."

Circe's Island

King Alcinous patted Ulysses on the back.

"Well done!" he said, "an excellent story, and very well told. But tell us what happened next, and how you almost got back to Ithaca."

"Yes, tell us some more!" shouted someone from the back of the hall.

"But your majesty, isn't it getting rather late?" protested Ulysses, smiling. In fact, he loved talking about his adventures, but it wouldn't be polite to carry on all night.

"Nonsense! The night is young!" cried Alcinous, who had now recovered completely from his queasiness. "Go on, sir, do!"

"Well," said Ulysses, "if that's what you want..."

There was a ripple of enthusiastic agreement through the hall, and Ulysses began.

"After our encounter with the Cyclops," he said, "we sailed on miserably, grieving for our lost friends. But the next place we came to gave us, at last, a proper welcome.

"It was the home of Aeolus, who is, I must admit, rather strange. There he lives, in the lap of luxury, on the floating island of Aeolia. He and his wife have six daughters and six sons, and they're all married to each other! But I warned my men not to remark on it, of course. People say Aeolus is a friend of the gods.

"Well, Aeolus entertained us splendidly with wonderful food and wine, in exchange for news about what happened at Troy. And when it was time for us to leave, he said he had a gift for me. 'Just a little something, to help you on your way,' he said. And do you know what it was?"

The guests in the hall leaned closer.

"A bag of winds," said Ulysses proudly. "The best present any seafarer could have. He presented me with this huge sack, which was bouncing and buffeting around as if it were full of fighting puppies. Inside, Aeolus had trapped the power of all the four

winds for us to use on our journey, and tied the bag with a silver string.

"I really couldn't thank him enough!" said Ulysses. "But now that we had the winds, my men were eager to get back. So off we went. We had no problem sailing straight for Ithaca, and within a few days there we were at last, within sight of the shore..."

Ulysses's voice trailed off. He looked heartbroken. "It was so beautiful," he said, quietly. "We could see the people on the rocky beaches, tending their fires and waving to us. Behind them, the dark peak of Mount Neriton rose into the sky. It had been nearly eleven years since I'd seen it.

"I was so happy, and so relieved, that I felt I could relax at last. I lay down to rest on the deck while my men rowed us to land. And there I fell asleep. A fatal mistake.

"While I was snoozing on the deck, some of the men started wondering what other presents from Aeolus might be in the bag. 'I bet he's given him a pile of gold and silver, and he doesn't want to share it with us!' one of the men reportedly said, and eventually they all agreed to have a look. What a disaster! As soon as they opened the bag, the four winds got out and immediately produced a storm which blew us right back the way we'd come."

"I was woken up by my men calling out in anguish, as they saw their beloved homeland vanishing into the distance. But by then, there was nothing I could do. The storm took hold, and I've never seen one like it in my life. It sank eleven of the twelve ships in my fleet. My own crew spent hours dragging shipwrecked men from the other boats out of the water. But I'm afraid many of them drowned.

"So, with an overcrowded ship, and most of the men so exhausted and depressed they were just about useless, we limped back into Aeolus's island.

"I felt pretty stupid, I can tell you. I thought he might help us out, but he was furious. 'You timewasters!' he snorted, 'I gave you every possible chance. If you can't manage to get home even with a bag of winds, you must be cursed by the gods, and I don't want you hanging around! Be off with you!' And that was that."

"We were back to square one, traipsing from one place to another, and wondering how we'd ever get home again. And you can imagine that by now, my men were begging me not to explore any more. It seemed that everywhere we went we found trouble in one form or another. So when we stopped on a little forested island, I knew the wisest thing would be to stay on the shore, rest for a while, and then get going again.

"But as usual I just couldn't resist it. I left them all asleep on the beach and climbed a nearby hill. And what did I see? A wisp of smoke, rising from a mountainside right in the middle of the island. I had to investigate.

"I went back and woke them up. They protested, but I was their leader, and complaining didn't do them any good. To make it fair, I split us into two groups – I was in charge of one, and I put Eurylochus in charge of the other. Then we drew straws, and Eurylochus's group got the job of finding out where that smoke was coming from.

"He told me later what had happened. On the steep hillside, in the middle of the forest, next to a clear mountain stream, they'd found a charming little stone cottage. Prowling around it were real wolves and lions, drugged with something to make them docile. Instead of biting the men, they jumped up and licked their faces, like big, friendly dogs.

"Through the doorway of the house they could see a beautiful woman with green eyes. They immediately recognized her as Circe, the sorceress, daughter of the sun god, Helios. She was weaving an everlasting magical cloth, and singing to herself.

"Well, as soon as she noticed them she invited them inside. They were so impressed by her beauty, and by her soft, purring voice, that they all trooped right in. Only Eurylochus, who suspected some kind of a trap, stayed behind. He waited in the garden, keeping a watchful eye on those slavering beasts."

"Inside, Circe offered the men a local delicacy to refresh them: a mixture of cheese, honey and barley soaked in wine. But there was something else in it too. The minute they'd eaten it, up got Circe and

used her wand to poke and drive them out of the door. They'd all been turned into pigs! They had human feelings all right, but they looked and sounded like pigs. They even smelled like them, Eurylochus told me.

"The next thing he knew, Circe was shooing them all through the yard. She penned them all up in a pigsty, and Eurylochus came running back through the woods in desperation to find me.

"He wasn't too pleased about it, either. 'Ulysses!' he shouted, as he ran panting onto the beach, 'now you've done it! Everywhere we go, your curiosity just gets more of our men killed. Or turned into pigs!' he added, 'because that's what happened! This is Circe's island! You've led us right into a witch's den!'

"I had to go and try to help my men," said Ulysses, "even though the others pleaded with me just to set sail and abandon them. Off I went, tearing through the undergrowth, intent on doing something about Circe and getting our men back, when I ran head on into Hermes, the messenger of the gods.

" 'Hermes! What on earth are you doing here?' I panted.

" 'At your service,' he grinned. I stopped and caught my breath. The handsome young god sat down on a log and put his feet up on a rock.

" 'I'm here to help you deal with Circe. I'm assuming you don't want to be turned into a pig too,' he said casually.

"I hadn't thought of that. 'Well, no,' I admitted.

" 'All right then,' he said, and he pulled this great big bush out of the ground and broke a piece off. It wasn't really necessary to uproot it, but the gods are so strong, they can do anything.

" 'Here's what you must do,' he said. 'Eat this herb, It's called moly. When you meet Circe, she'll feed you drugged food, but the moly will protect you. After you've eaten, draw your sword and threaten to kill her. She'll beg for mercy. Make her promise not to harm you, and you'll have her in your power.'

"Well, it sounded easy enough," said Ulysses, "so I thanked Hermes, and set off for Circe's house."

"Circe was waiting for me as I walked into the clearing and stepped past the drugged animals. She really was amazingly beautiful – tall, with long, dark hair, and large, clear green eyes, like a snake's. She was

slowly looking me up and down with that bewitching stare.

" 'Come in, come in, my darling,' she said, in a soft, low, purring voice. But I didn't find it very romantic. I was too scared.

"She invited me to sit on a decorated silver chair while she prepared me some dinner. I could see her mixing things into it, but I didn't say anything. I ate it all.

"She stood up and prodded me with her wand.

"I waited, fearful that at any second I would turn into a pig.

"But nothing happened. I wasn't a pig. The moly had worked! I was quite surprised myself, actually. Then I remembered the next part of the plan, and quickly drew my sword. 'Circe!' I shouted, rushing at her, 'Give me back my crewmen, or I'll cut your throat!'

"She crumpled onto the floor and flung her arms around my legs in terror. 'Who are you?' she cried. 'No one has ever resisted my magic before!' "

"But then a change came over her. Her snake eyes narrowed, and she started to look very cunning. 'I know who you must be,' she said slinkily, starting to rub my leg. 'Only the famous Ulysses, the cleverest, boldest... and most handsome of warriors,' she smiled, 'could possibly survive the drug that turns men into pigs. Oh Ulysses, is it you?' she wheedled. 'Please, stay with me for a while, and we can live together like a husband and wife.'

"It was embarrassing," Ulysses admitted, "but also flattering. And she was very good-looking. I was just starting to think about accepting, when I remembered my men, shut up in the pigsty.

" 'Circe,' I said, trying to sound forceful, 'how do you expect me to trust you when you have turned my men into pigs? Turn them back immediately, and promise me you won't harm any of us. Then maybe I'll think about it.'

" 'Oh, Ulysses, you're so manly,' she purred, getting up. Then she leaned over to me and stroked my face softly, looking deep into my eyes. I tried to look away.

" 'It's a deal,' she said at last. 'I'll set the men free and promise not to hurt anyone, as long as you, my gorgeous warrior, promise to stay with me. For a year.'

"I had no choice. I had to agree – I didn't want to. But she led me out to the pig pen, and using her magic wand, prodded and poked the pigs so that their bristles fell off, their snouts shrank and, one by one, they were transformed into upright men again. They wept with joy to see each other, and I knew I'd done the right thing.

"And so I brought the others up from the beach, and we all had to stay with Circe for year.

"After her promise, she no longer had any power to trick us. And I must say, we had quite a pleasant time there," said Ulysses, blushing. "Certainly, if I hadn't met Circe, I would never have found out how to get home. Or rather," he added, "how to get this far. For I still haven't set foot on Ithaca since I left for Troy, nineteen years ago."

"That day shall soon come," said King Alcinous. "We can only show our gratitude to such a master storyteller by taking you safely home tomorrow. But tonight," he announced, "we shall hear some more of your tale."

"Yes, Ulysses," said Queen Arete, "what exactly did Circe teach you? How did you find out how to get back? Where did you go next?"

"Of all the places I've been to," said Ulysses, "the next one was the most frightening. I've met a lot of people. But there was one race I never thought I'd meet. Not until I'd fallen in battle, drowned at sea, or grown old and died by my own hearth, did I ever think I would talk to the dead.

"Here I am before you – living, breathing and strong, thanks to your excellent dinner! But I, Ulysses," – his hushed voice echoed gently through the hall – "I have been down to Hades, where the dead lie moaning for evermore. And I've survived to tell the tale."

The Land of the Dead

"The year passed," began Ulysses, "and I knew I'd have to say something to Circe. I found her weaving in her usual way, but the expression on her face showed me she knew what was coming. When I told her it was time for us to go, she looked very annoyed.

" 'How do you think you're going to make it home, then?" she asked, resentfully. I hadn't even thought about it. All I could say was, 'Well... we'll just set off, and hope for better luck.'

" 'There's only one way to make sure of a safe return,' said Circe, looking at me as if I was an idiot. 'You must go and see Teiresias, the soothsayer.'

" 'But Teiresias is dead!' I protested.

" 'Even the dead have a home,' she answered, and I realized what she was saying.

"If I was going to get Teiresias's advice, I would have to go to Hades itself... the Land of the Dead," Ulysses whispered, eerily. The hall had grown dark, and the servants were lighting lamps. The guests' wide-eyed faces glowed in the orange light.

"Circe told me how to get there. She told me to set sail and follow the current to the south, then go up the River of Ocean. Where two streams met, I was to dig a small trench and sacrifice a black ewe and a white ram, so that their blood filled the trench.

"Then, she promised, the shadowy ghosts of the dead would rise out of the ground. 'But keep them away with your sword!' she warned. 'Don't let them drink the blood until Teiresias has had his turn!'

I went to tell the men to get ready to go. And even then, it seemed, we couldn't leave without a tragedy. Some of the crew were taking a nap in the sun on Circe's roof. And when I called to them, one young lad, Elpenor, forgot where he was, stumbled and fell off, breaking his neck.

"Elpenor always was a bit clumsy. But I couldn't help wondering if the heartless sea god Poseidon didn't have something to do with our endless string of catastrophes."

"Anyway, it wasn't long before we found ourselves sailing into the swirling mouth of the River of Ocean, away from the open sea. Circe had summoned up a wind to take us there.

"But as we progressed inland, everything became strangely quiet. There was no wind, and the water was flat calm. All around, the land was low and dark, covered with a creeping, greenish mist. Our ship just seemed to push its way onward, slowly, magically, on and on, through the unearthly silence, into the Kingdom of Decay.

"We moored where Circe had told us to, and started walking across the swampy ground, dragging with us the ram and ewe for sacrificing. Their bleats were the only sounds. The mist swirled around our shins as we came to the place where two streams joined. There, I fell on my knees and started digging a trench in the marshy soil with my dagger.

"We were trembling by the time we came to sacrifice the sheep. Eurylochus and Polites held them still while I slit their throats, turning my head away to face the River of Ocean, as Circe had instructed. The animals fell to the ground and their blood overflowed the little trench I had dug.

"We waited, staring hard into the mist.

"There was a low, murmuring sound, which grew into a quiet whimpering and moaning. Suddenly, I thought I could make out a face forming in the green shadows. But it wasn't Teiresias.

"It was my mother, Anticleia."

"I had no idea that she had died while I'd been gone. 'Mother!' I cried out to her, but suddenly her face had become one of hundreds of moving, shifting, fluttering figures, filling the air around us. They were rising out of the ground faster and faster, armies of young soldiers with gaping spear wounds, brides struck down on their wedding day, children who had fallen sick, and old, withered men and women, with life's suffering behind them.

"Their horrible moaning and green, decaying faces made me panic with fear. I felt the blood drain away from my face, and I thought I was about to faint, when I remembered that I must stop the dead from reaching the blood. Some of them were already creeping and swirling over to it.

"I grabbed my sword and held it shakily in front of the trench. 'Teiresias?' I called out. My voice sounded like a whimpering kitten. 'Teiresias, where are you?' I called again, feeling the panic rising in my throat.

"An old, bent figure could be seen feeling its way forward.

" 'Royal son of Laertes,' croaked Teiresias. His blind eyes roamed blankly upward. 'Allow me to drink, so that I may foresee your future.'

"Then he bent down, and I stepped back, terrified of being touched by his misty form. As he drank the warm blood, he began to look more solid, and his voice became more human.

" 'Oh, Teiresias,' I began, nervously. In one way, I didn't want to know my future. No man wants to know the date of his own death. But I needed to know if we would get home, and how.

" 'Please tell me what... what will become of me,' I begged him.

"I felt like a coward. Me, Ulysses, reduced to a quivering wreck in front of a blind old man, terrified of my own death. For death, after all, comes to everyone, and a warrior should not be afraid," Ulysses reminded his audience in the hall.

"Anyway, Teiresias gave me as full an answer as anyone could wish for. This is what he told me.

" 'My Lord Ulysses, you are hoping for an easy way home. But Poseidon will fill your days with danger. He has not forgotten that you blinded his beloved son, the Cyclops. Nevertheless, you and your crew may get home safely, if you follow my advice.

" 'You will come to the Island of the Sun, where the sun god Helios tends his sturdy cattle. Whatever you do,' – and here Teiresias waved a bony finger at me – 'whatever you do, you must not kill the sheep and oxen of the Sun. Leave them untouched, and you will get home. But if a single one of the Sun's animals is killed, you may never return. Or if you do, you will arrive late, after years of misery, on an unknown ship, with all your comrades dead, and trouble brewing in your royal house!'

"I shivered, realizing that these were the exact same words the Cyclops had used when he called on his father Poseidon to curse me. But Teiresias was about to speak again.

" 'For when you do get home,' he went on, 'you'll find the place full of scoundrels trying to persuade your wife to marry them, and abusing the hospitality of your son, Telemachus. You'll have to fight them, Ulysses. And even when you've dealt with them, you'll have more journeys to make.

" 'But for you, I predict a happy end. After a peaceful old age, death will come to you out of the sea, in a gentle disguise. This is the truth that I have told you...'

"Teiresias was starting to fade away. He was becoming misty at the edges.

" 'Teiresias!' I called to him. 'There's one more thing! I saw my mother here, among the dead. How can I speak to her?'

"Teiresias had almost turned back into a swirl of green mist, but I heard him calling: 'The blood, Ulysses. You may speak to any of the dead, but they must drink the blood...'

"I looked down at the murky pool of sheep's blood in the trench. How could I ask my mother to drink that?

" 'Mother?' I ventured. 'Mother!'

"She came up to me, out of the crowds of the dead. Her fluttering, shadowy form knelt down and drank at the trench, and she stood up looking almost more solid and strong than when I had last seen her alive. 'Mother!' I cried, stepping forward and flinging my arms around her.

"But my arms closed on nothing.

" 'Oh, Ulysses, my darling son!' she cried, 'I am not made of flesh, and you cannot touch me. When we come here, our bodies decay. This is only my spirit that stands before you. My darling, where have you been? Why didn't you come home? And if you're still alive, why are you in Hades?'

" 'I have still not been home,' I answered her. 'It seems I'm destined to wander all over the world. I came here to ask Teiresias about my future. But Mother, what happened in Ithaca? How did you die?'

" 'I died of grief for my lost son,' she wept. I could see tears well up in her eyes and trickle down her cheeks, but still I couldn't touch and comfort her.

" 'I am alive and safe, Mother,' I reassured her. I didn't tell her what Teiresias had said about the difficult challenges ahead of me. 'Tell me... how is Penelope? And my father? And Telemachus,' I pleaded. 'Tell me how he has grown up.'

" 'Penelope's a good girl, and I'm sure she'll wait for you,' she said, absent-mindedly. 'Your father spends his time on the farm, away from the palace. It takes his mind off his troubles,' she added, dabbing at her tears. 'But Telemachus — oh, Ulysses, you would be proud. He looks so much like you, and I know he's going to grow up just as strong and brave as you are. But it's been hard for him, without a father. You must go back, Ulysses. Hurry back to the land of daylight, before it's too late!'

"My mother faded away, and I was left staring into the clouds of green mist. I was about to tell my companions we should go back, when I noticed that another green, shadowy form was at my feet, bending forward to drink the blood. I could see from his broad shoulders that this time it was a man, cut down by some disease or disaster in the prime of life."

"As it drained the trench to the bottom, the ghost took on a solid shape, and slowly stood up before me. I was flabbergasted.

"I recognized those laughing eyes, the broad chest and friendly face of the man who'd been my closest companion at Troy. I desperately wanted to hug him — to throw my arms around him, to slap him on the back and shake him by the hand. But I couldn't.

" 'Agamemnon!' I gasped. 'How... ? What... ? I thought you were alive! What happened?'

"The laughing light in his eyes dimmed a little as Agamemnon cast his eyes down, almost with shame.

" 'I was killed,' he admitted. 'Well... murdered.'

" 'But... not at Troy!' I protested. 'You left with me! I saw you sailing off for home. Surely you made it?'

" 'Yes...' Agamemnon looked pained. 'My wife, Clytemnestra. And her... her lover, Aegisthus. They were waiting for me when I got home.'

" 'Oh, Agamemnon, that's terrible!' I said, awkwardly. I didn't know how to comfort him. My best friend, and one of the greatest warriors in the world, murdered by his own wife and her lover!

" 'After surviving Troy, and everything!' I went on. 'To get home, and... and have that happen.'

" 'I know,' agreed Agamemnon, grimacing apologetically. He looked up at me. 'I'm telling you, Ulysses. Don't trust women. Never, ever put your trust in a woman. Look what happened to me.'

" 'But Penelope wouldn't...' I faltered.

" 'Don't you believe it!' said Agamemnon. 'You heard Teiresias. Even now your house is full of fancy men, all with their eye on your queen. And Ulysses,' he whispered, 'women are weak. She won't hold out forever. Take my advice — be prepared. Don't walk straight into a trap like I did. When you get back, you'll have to think of a plan to get rid of them.'

"As he spoke, he too began to fade, and the eerie moaning of the other ghosts grew louder. Suddenly there seemed to be even more of them, crowding and fluttering around us. My fear caught up with me again, and I was terrified that some monster, like the terrible gorgon, might rise up out of the ground and destroy us. We stumbled backward. Then we turned and ran for our boat, leaving the legions of the dead sinking slowly, wailing, back into the ground."

"But just as we were about to reach the ship, we became aware of another ghost in our path. It was a forlorn figure, his head hanging to one side.

" 'Elpenor!' gasped Eurylochus. It was the oarsman who'd fallen off the roof. He didn't need to drink the blood before he could speak.

" 'My friends, help me!' he called out. 'I am not living, and I am not dead. When you hurried away from Circe's island, you forgot to bury me, and I cannot rest in peace!'

"We gazed in horror at his decaying flesh, his hollow eyes, and his neck, twisted and hanging slack where he had broken it.

" 'You must go back to the island and bury me!'

"We quickly embarked, cut loose the ropes, and let the River of Ocean carry us swiftly out to sea.

"We couldn't let Elpenor suffer the life of a zombie. We had to go back to Circe's island. And it was just as well we did. When Elpenor's body had been put to rest, and we were ready to leave, the beautiful goddess took me to one side.

" 'Ulysses,' she purred, 'what amazing courage! By visiting the Land of the Dead, you've proved yourself the bravest of men. But let me tell you,' she added, drawing closer to me, 'there are more problems lined up for you. And only I can tell you what they are.'

" 'My fair goddess,' I replied politely, 'Teiresias did explain to me about the sheep and oxen of the Sun.'

" 'But did he tell you about the ladies who are lying in wait?' she asked, enigmatically. 'Ulysses, I think I may have very some useful advice for you. Just stay with me for one more night, and... well,' she said, winking slyly, 'I'll teach you all I know.'

"Well," said Ulysses to the sniggering guests, "that seemed like a fair exchange, and after all, it's always better to set sail in the morning.

"So we stayed one more night, and Circe warned me about the dangers that lay around the corner: the Sirens, beautiful yet evil monsters, who would try to lure us to our deaths; and Scylla, the many-headed monster, with rows of sharp teeth, who would try to snatch men screaming from the deck.

"These horrors were yet to come. And without Circe's advice, I would never have survived."

The Island of the Sun

"By the time we finally set off from Circe's island, the crew had recovered their spirits and were excited about getting home. But I was full of a sense of foreboding," Ulysses told Alcinous and his guests. "And my instincts were right. It was to be our most dangerous journey yet."

"But surely, you were on your way home," said King Alcinous. "After all, Teiresias and Circe had warned you about all the dangers."

"Yes," said Ulysses, "well, I knew how to get past the Sirens, but I hadn't even told the crew about Scylla. I didn't know how to. The truth was, Circe had said there was no way we'd get past Scylla without losing at least six men. I told her I was prepared to fight the monster, but she just laughed. She assured me that no mere mortal – not even me! – could fight that six-headed monster."

Ulysses sighed. "I should have told them," he said through gritted teeth, angry at his own cowardice. "But I wanted to get home as quickly as possible. There was also the little matter of not killing those animals when we reached the Island of the Sun. It sounded easy enough, but I had a nasty feeling I wasn't going to be able to control things. I decided it would be better to avoid the island altogether. I was sitting on the deck, thinking about what to do, when Eurylochus hurried up and tapped me on the shoulder.

" 'Sir,' he said, shaking me out of my daydream, 'what are those islands ahead? I've never seen such an eerie-looking spot, sir! Should we turn back?'

"And there they were ahead of us, the needle-sharp, cruelly jagged rocks where the Sirens live. Some people think the Sirens are just mythical creatures, but they're not."

All the guests listening to Ulysses's tale had heard stories about the deadly Sirens, but none had actually seen them. People said that no one had ever sailed past them and lived to tell the tale. And yet here before them was a man who said he had. The guests were even more amazed than ever.

"Oh yes," went on Ulysses, "they look just like beautiful women, singing on the shore. But they're evil. They call out to passing sailors, singing the most beautiful, hypnotic music in the world. It makes you go mad with desire, but when you try to get nearer, SMASH! You hit those fatal, jagged rocks – and that's exactly what they want. Well, I wasn't going to let that happen to me.

" 'It's too late to turn back!' I shouted to the men. 'Quick – we must follow Circe's instructions.' The men gathered around me while I feverishly tried to roll and soften a lump of beeswax between my palms. I pinched off a piece of wax for each man to plug his ears with. But I wanted to hear the Sirens singing, so I asked the men to tie me firmly to the mast, as Circe had advised. They'd just finished tying the last rope when I heard the first strains of music floating on the breeze.

"The men went about their work, but I was absolutely transfixed. That music – the singing – I can't describe it. It was like – like the taste of honey and sparkling wine mixed together. It was like being tickled with a feather all the way down your spine. It was as if the air had turned golden and silver. But no... it was even more beautiful than that. Those soft, soaring, intertwined voices... it was so beautiful, I just longed to, had to hear more of it. I couldn't bear the thought of our ship sailing on past those rocks... the thought of never hearing that incredible sound again...

"So I tried to catch my men's attention, which wasn't exactly easy, because they were all temporarily completely deaf.

"I motioned to them to untie me – I didn't care what happened to them any more, as long as I could stay with the Sirens for ever.

"But they knew what to do. They were such a good crew," said Ulysses, drifting off into a sad reverie for his old comrades. "I still can't believe I'll never see them again."

"What? What did they do?" asked Queen Arete.

"They tied me on tighter, of course!" replied Ulysses. "And it was just as well. As we rounded the rocks, we came to the highest, most jagged pinnacle of all. And piled up on it, like the remains of yesterday's dinner, were the bones. Hundreds of human bones, picked white by the seagulls, and speckled with slimy green moss – skulls and skeletons of seafarers, like me, lured to their deaths. We'd had a narrow escape."

"Soon, the Sirens' voices faded, and there I was, tied to the mast, wondering why I'd been such an

idiot. Seeing that I was back to normal, the men unplugged their ears and untied me. We sat down and started congratulating ourselves on our escape. And then, almost immediately, I saw the two rocks of Scylla and Charybdis poking out of the water like huge, pointing grey fingers. I could hardly believe it."

"What are Scylla and Charybdis?" asked the bard, Demodocus. "Why would anyone be afraid of two rocks?"

"The rocks merely mark the spot," Ulysses answered him gravely, "where thousands of men have lost their lives. A strong current forces every sailor to pass between them. On one side, the rock is flat and hard, rising straight up out of the sea. And there, in a cave, halfway up, lives Scylla. Of all the monsters I've ever seen, she was the most terrifying.

"Six heads," Ulysses whispered, peering from one face to another in the darkened hall, "each one on the end of a long, snaky neck. And on each head, three rows of long, pointed teeth, like a shark's. Circe had warned me that Scylla could dart out of her hole in half a second, and that her necks were long enough to reach anyone on the deck. But, Circe said, it was better to sail close to Scylla's rock and risk losing a few men than to go too near Charybdis, the powerful whirlpool, which would suck all of us and our ship down in an instant.

" 'All hands on deck!' I cried. 'Row between the rocks, but keep close to the left-hand one, to avoid the whirlpool.'

"My closest comrade Eurylochus turned to me. 'Whirlpool?' he asked, looking horrified.

" 'There's nothing to worry about,' I lied to the panicking men who were crowding around me. 'Circe told me we'll be fine as long as we keep close to the left-hand rock on the way through. All hands on deck!'

"So the men set to work, rowing us nearer to the tall, spooky grey fingers of stone. I stared up at the left one to see if I could spot Scylla crouching in her cave. But even though I peered at every inch of the rock's surface until my eyes hurt, I couldn't see any cave at all, let alone any sign of the monster. I began to think maybe it was our lucky day, and Scylla wasn't at home."

"Suddenly I heard a loud sucking, belching sound to our right. I looked around. The men were staring in horror across to the opposite side of the channel.

"The sea had opened up into a huge, gaping, swirling vortex. Faster, deeper and darker it spun, until we could peer down into it, and even catch a glimpse of the wet, sandy floor of the ocean itself. It was like looking over the edge of a cliff made of spinning, swirling water. Then, just as suddenly as it had opened, the whirlpool collapsed in on itself with a resounding slap, forcing an enormous plume of water up into the sky. It surged up even higher than the rocks themselves, showering our deck with salt water. The men cowered in terror.

" 'See,' I said, trying to reassure them. 'We're out of its range. Row on, and we'll make it through safely. Row on!' And the men strained at the oars, dragging us through the water, scraping close by Scylla's rock. But everyone's eyes were fixed on the massive, bubbling whirlpool, which was beginning to boil and swirl around for a second time.

"Then I heard a quick, hissing, flapping sound, and heard the agonized cry of Polites, one of my best oarsmen. I spun around. Scylla's heads were among us, darting this way and that around the deck like serpents. Her scaly, writhing necks coiled and twisted out of a cleft high up in the rock. The heads snapped and grabbed at the men, who tried to fend them off with their oar handles, and the air was filled with this awful, strangled hissing sound. Instinctively, my hand reached for my sword. But I remembered Circe's words: no mere mortal can fight that six-headed monster. There was nothing I could do.

"The first head was raised above us, and clamped firmly between its rows of teeth was poor Polites, bleeding and screaming. Soon the other heads had each caught a helpless oarsmen and lifted them way above us, kicking, struggling and shrieking, until they disappeared into the rock face. We heard a disgusting crunching, slurping sound. Then nothing but the regular slap of the waves on the sides of the boat, and the belching of the whirlpool.

"I looked back down into the boat. The horrified faces of the rest of the men stared blankly at me.

" 'Row on,' I ordered, shakily. 'Let's get ourselves out of here.'

"Grim-faced, some of them with tears rolling down their cheeks, the men rowed determinedly on until we were clear of that horrible place.

"After that, I could hardly deny them a rest. They were terrified, exhausted and traumatized. So I said we could moor for the night. We'd come to a nice little low-lying island and dragged the ship ashore before I realized where we were. And then I began to feel uncomfortable."

"There was something about the place that made me sure it was the Island of the Sun. It was partly the sheep and cows that were wandering around. They were just too perfect. They were all strong and large, with broad foreheads, thick, glossy coats and big, solid horns. Not a single one of them was lame, small or

dirty. It was as if they were gods among animals. And the light – everything was suffused in a golden-pink glow, like sunlight in the late evening. It was a truly beautiful place. But I was worried.

" 'Comrades,' I announced, 'You know Teiresias predicted we would come to the Island of the Sun. I think this is it, and...'

" 'Don't worry,' said Eurylochus in exasperation. 'We'll just eat our own rations. We won't touch a single sheep or cow. You can trust us!'

"But still, I made every single man promise not to kill any of the Sun's cattle, before I would sit down to supper."

"It would have been fine," lamented Ulysses. "We had plenty of rations, and no one was in a mood to annoy the sun god, or any other god for that matter. The only thing we all wanted to get home as soon as possible. But that bully Poseidon still found a way to cause trouble.

"He sent us a storm, didn't he? The whole island was lashed by gales and huge waves, and we couldn't possibly set off in that. It carried on for a week. Then another week. A month after we'd arrived, it was still blowing a gale, and we were running out of supplies. I told the men they could try to catch fish if they wanted, but they were not, under any circumstances, to kill the sheep or cows. And with that, I left them at our camp on the beach while I went to find somewhere to pray.

"I tramped inland through the dripping wet undergrowth, feeling furious, but trying to control myself. I needed to pray to all the gods – including Poseidon – if I was going to make any difference.

"After a while I came to a temple in the middle of the woods, and I knew I'd been right about where we were. It was the sun god's temple, and this was definitely his island. I stepped inside, wiping my feet and trying to shake the worst of the rainwater off my clothes in the entrance hall, before going anxiously up to the altar.

"I kneeled down and tried to calm my nerves. All I could hear was the hammering of the rain outside, and the thumping of my own heart."

" 'Lord Zeus, mighty ruler of the sky,' I began. 'And Helios, glowing god of the sun. Gorgeous Athene of the flashing eyes! Hermes, handsome messenger, and all the other wise and beautiful gods who live on Mount Olympus! And, er, Poseidon,' I added. 'Please, please stop this storm, so that we can sail home safely.'

"Then, summoning up all my willpower, I prayed silently, willing my message to fly up to the gods. Perhaps they would send me a sign. But nothing happened, except that an old goblet on the altar toppled over and rolled onto the floor, breaking in half.

"I don't know if that was a bad omen, but I decided to ignore it. I'd done my best. So I set off through the rain, back to the beach, to try to cheer up my comrades.

"But as I tramped down the last stretch of grass onto the sandy shore, I smelled something that made me realize my worst fears had come true. It was a smell that would normally cheer me up, but now it made my stomach lurch and my head spin. It was the warm, familiar aroma of roasting beef."

" 'NO-OOOOOO!' I screamed, running down over the green grass, over the golden sand, and wrenching the blackened carcass of the cow off the spit the men had built. But it was far too late. I slumped down on the damp beach and covered my face with my hands. 'We're ruined!' I groaned. Flashing through my mind were the fateful words the Cyclops and Teiresias had used...You will come home late... on an unknown ship... all your comrades dead... trouble brewing... trouble brewing...

" 'Better to take whatever the gods throw at us than die a lingering death from malnutrition!' said Eurylochus indignantly. 'We had to do it! We'd have starved to death otherwise!'

" 'Don't eat it!' I wailed, 'Don't eat it!' But they were already tucking hungrily into the perfectly roasted flesh of the cow they had killed. I was the only one who refused to eat the meat.

"Then, something really strange happened. Although there were no other cows nearby, we heard a long, low, mooing sound. We couldn't tell where it was coming from. But it got louder and louder, until it felt as if a cow was mooing right in my ear. We clapped our hands over our ears and ran to hide behind some bushes. And peering out from behind them, we saw the leathery hide of the dead animal begin to move from where the men had cast it aside. It got up slowly, and half-limped, half-wobbled around, like a new-born calf, making this terrible, eerie mooing noise. This really was a bad omen from the gods, I knew that much.

"At last it went and lay down again, exactly where it had been before. When we eventually came out from behind the bushes, some of the men managed to convince themselves they'd imagined it. They went ahead and helped themselves to more meat, seeming completely carefree, while I went down and sat by the waves and prayed as hard as I could, knowing all the time that there was no longer anything I could do."

"Soon after that, the storm died down, and the next day I ordered my men to prepare the ship for sea once more. We set sail, but I had an even greater sense of foreboding than before, and I was hardly surprised when, as soon as we were out of sight of any land, the sky darkened and fat, heavy drops of rain began plopping onto the deck. Then the waves became rougher, and the raindrops were replaced by huge, deadly hailstones. On top of that, a hurricane-force wind suddenly hit us from the north. We all manned the oars, trying to guide the ship out of trouble, screaming instructions at each other through the blasting wind and hail.

"But even above the noise of the storm, I was aware of the slow, creaking sound of the mast beginning to topple. It gathered momentum and crashed down onto the deck, hitting the helmsman on the back of the head and splitting open his skull. He dropped off the front of the ship and plunged like a stone into the billowing waves. And just as he hit the water, a shaft of lightning sent by Zeus crashed out of the sky and scored a direct hit. I don't think there was anything accidental about it. The sun god must have been furious with us."

"The boat exploded into a thousand fragments. We were all flung far out into the black, roaring sea. I only managed to stay afloat by clinging onto a piece of wood. All of the others drowned."

Ulysses shook his head sadly. A murmur of sympathy ran round the hall.

"For nine days I floated helplessly in the rough seas, swallowing salt water, trying to stay conscious, and hallucinating that I was back home with my family in Ithaca. I only stayed alive by counting the sunrises and sunsets, making myself watch the stars at night and the patterns of clouds by day.

"When, at last, I felt two soft, strong arms pull me from a shallow bay, and heard the soft whispering of a woman, I dreamed it was Penelope.

"But it was Calypso, the nymph. She rescued me, but she held me prisoner too. It was seven long years before I was able to escape to this wonderful place." Ulysses surveyed the hall, the empty dinner plates, and the astounded faces of the guests, and reminded himself how lucky he was to be alive.

Coming Home

Ulysses's tale was finished. There was complete silence as he looked around the shadowy hall at his audience. They stared back at him, each person wondering at the astonishing things Ulysses had seen and the horrors he had survived.

Then the gentle sound of snoring was heard drifting from the back of the hall. Ulysses smiled awkwardly. "I'm sorry to have kept you all awake," he apologized.

"It was worth it," said King Alcinous. "That was the best story I've ever heard. And we are very lucky to have such a great hero as yourself here to entertain us. However," he yawned, getting up from his throne, "it is extremely late. I propose we all go to bed, and tomorrow the best oarsmen in Phaeacia will take you home, carrying the most precious gifts Phaeacia can provide, in return for your excellent tale."

The next day, King Alcinous chose some expensive bronze bowls, precious jewels, and beautiful silk clothing embroidered with silver thread as presents for Ulysses. He took them down to the ship himself and stowed them under the rowing benches, while Queen Arete sent her servants to load the ship with bread and wine for the oarsmen.

The sun was sinking in the west by the time everything was prepared. Ulysses watched patiently, itching to get going, as the oarsmen carried a soft rug and blanket onto the deck for him to sleep on. He turned to the crowd standing on the beach, the king and queen with their crowns gleaming in the evening light, and their beautiful daughter, Nausicaa, who had rescued him and brought him to the palace.

"My friends," he announced, "may your country be blessed, and may you live in happiness forever! Thank you for all you have done for me. And thank you, Nausicaa, for your kindness. I hope you find a wonderful husband!"

With that, the crowd erupted into cheers, Nausicaa blushed, and Ulysses stepped on board. He waved to the excited people as the oarsmen heaved on the oars and the ship pulled slowly out of the bay.

Then, exhausted after the previous evening's performance, Ulysses climbed into his makeshift bed on the deck. As he slept, the ship gathered speed and sliced through the dark water on its way to Ithaca.

"Where am I?" mumbled Ulysses sleepily.

It was dawn. Ulysses was lying on his rug, under his blanket, which was speckled with dew, on an unfamiliar beach. His breath formed clouds in the cold early morning air, and all around, a thick mist shrouded the landscape.

"Oh no!" said Ulysses angrily, sitting up. "It's happened again! I always think I'm about to make it back to Ithaca, and I always end up miles from anywhere."

Then Ulysses noticed a pile of precious bronzeware and jewels sparkling in the sunlight nearby – his presents from King Alcinous. What was going on?

"Ulysses," came a woman's voice from behind him. "You're not going to give up now, I hope, not now that you're back in Ithaca."

"Athene!" Ulysses spun around. There she stood, tall, beautiful and radiant, with a mocking look in her eyes, her hands on her hips, and her spear planted firmly in the sand beside her.

"But this isn't Ithaca!" Ulysses blustered. "It doesn't look like it to me, anyhow. Where are the rocky fields full of sheep? Where's Mount Neriton? How did I get here?"

"The Phaeacians dropped you off," answered the goddess simply. "You were sleeping, so they left you here. And I didn't want you waking up and storming into town, half asleep, and announcing you were back. Ulysses, those suitors would have your guts for garters! They'd kill you on the spot! So, I disguised Ithaca."

As she spoke, the mist gradually disappeared, and Mount Neriton took shape, looming above them.

"Ithaca!" shouted Ulysses, hardly listening to her. "It is Ithaca. Oh Athene, I'm home. I'm home!" He grabbed handfuls of soft white sand and let them trickle through his fingers.

"Penelope! Telemachus! I must see them."

"No!" cut in Athene urgently. "Don't you remember what Teiresias warned you, and what the Cyclops wished on you? 'Trouble brewing in your royal house'?

"Ulysses, your palace is full of deadly enemies. Even now they are courting your wife Penelope. You've only just returned in time to stop her from choosing one of them as a husband – you must act quickly. But if you go alone, without preparation, they'll kill you. And that would be a waste of all your efforts to get home, wouldn't it?"

"The arrogant fools!" fumed Ulysses. "How dare they? I'll... I'll..." He stumbled upright, catching his foot in the blanket. "Where's my sword?"

"Ulysses," said Athene patiently. "Calm down. There's a better way. You're not going to defeat them without my help, so you might as well take my advice."

Ulysses looked annoyed. "I suppose so," he said.

"Now listen," said Athene. "I'm going to disguise you as an old beggar. Don't go to the city yet. Go and see Eumaeus, the swineherd, who's been loyal to you all this time. Stay in his hut until I tell you what to do. And don't tell anyone who you are." She picked up her spear. "I'm going to fetch Telemachus. He's gone off to Sparta to find out about you, and you'll need him here if there's going to be a battle. I'll tell him to come to Eumaeus's hut as well."

"Can I ask you something?" said Ulysses. "Why didn't you tell Telemachus where I was, and save him the journey?"

"He was better off away from those suitors," Athene answered. "Even now, they've sent a ship after him to try to ambush him. But don't worry," she added, seeing Ulysses's worried expression, "I'll see that he doesn't come to any harm."

Then she touched Ulysses with her spear, and shot off into the sky.

Ulysses looked down. He had the body of an old man, and instead of the spotless new tunic given to him by Nausicaa, he was wearing smelly, tattered rags. He felt his face. It was wrinkled and sagging. Ulysses hoped he wouldn't have to stay like this for long. But there was nothing he could do about it now. So, after hiding his presents in a cave, he set off for the pig farm to find Eumaeus.

Trudging up the hill to Eumaeus's hut, Ulysses caught sight of the old swineherd sitting on the garden wall, making himself a pair of leather sandals. After so many years away, Ulysses wanted to cry out to his faithful servant, "It's me, Ulysses!" But he stopped himself.

"Hello!" he shouted out instead, and was shocked to hear how old and croaky his voice sounded. "Any chance of a bed for the night?"

"Good day to you, sir! You look down on your luck, if you don't mind me saying so." called out Eumaeus. Ulysses was delighted to see how polite the swineherd was, even to an old beggar.

"You're welcome to share my hut, such as it is," Eumaeus went on regretfully. "It's not much of a place, I know. Time was when I'd have sent you down to the palace for a grander welcome. My old master King Ulysses, or his son Telemachus, they would have put you up in style. But now..." He shook his head. "Now, you'd probably just get a good old kicking. The place is full of young good-for-nothings!"

Ulysses opened his mouth to thank the swineherd for his hospitality, but Eumaeus went on, "I'm the swineherd, sir, you see. It's my job to rear pigs for the palace tables. But these days, I spend my time feeding my lady's suitors, as my master's been away for years."

"Thank you, sir, for your kind welcome," put in Ulysses quickly. "I must say, I'm a little hungry at the moment. Any chance of, er... ?"

"Of course, sir, where are my manners?" said Eumaeus, hopping off the wall in a surprisingly sprightly manner. "Do come inside for a bite to eat. I was just about to have breakfast myself. Nice day, isn't it?"

That evening, while Ulysses was tucking into his third meal of bread and pork of the day, Eumaeus explained that Telemachus had gone on a trip to look for his father.

"Strapping young lad," said Eumaeus approvingly. "Looks like his father, too. Anyway..."

His story was cut short by the appearance of a young man in the doorway. The evening sun shone from behind him, so Eumaeus and Ulysses could only see his silhouette. He was muscular and tall, with a long sword that glinted in the sunlight.

"Is that my young master?" ventured Eumaeus excitedly. "Back from abroad?" He got up and ran to the door, grasping Telemachus's hands in his.

"Oh sir, we thought we'd never see you again, after you slipped off in the night to look for your father! What on earth could you have been thinking of? You know those suitors were after you, don't you? But you're safe! The gods be thanked!"

He pulled Telemachus into the hut. "This is him!" he exclaimed to Ulysses. "This is my young master Telemachus! And this here," he said to Telemachus, "is a friend who's staying the night. Do sit down, sir, and I'll bring you something to eat. It's such a joy to see you – you hardly ever come up here to visit."

While Eumaeus bustled about in the tiny kitchen, Ulysses reached out to shake his son's hand, fighting back the lump in his throat. Telemachus's handshake was warm and strong. "You're very welcome to Ithaca, sir," he said. "I'm afraid my father's palace isn't fit for entertaining guests right now, but it's not our policy to turn away beggars. I'll have food and clothing sent up to you here."

"Thank you," was all Ulysses could manage.

Athene hadn't told Telemachus that Ulysses was at the hut. But she had told him to go there, and to send Eumaeus to the city to tell Penelope her son was home. That way, father and son would be left alone together. So, after they had spent the night around Eumaeus's fire, listening to Telemachus's tales of his journey, Eumaeus set off for the city.

"Tell only my mother I'm back!" Telemachus called after the old swineherd as he tramped down the hill. "No one else. I don't want those suitors finding out yet!"

Meanwhile, Ulysses had heard Athene's voice in his ear, "Meet me outside," she whispered. "At the back."

He found the goddess behind the hut. "The time has come," she whispered. Raising her spear, she transformed him back into his old self, strong, tall and handsome, with bright, rich clothing. "Go and introduce yourself to your son, so that together you can plot an attack on the suitors. I'll be back soon." And she disappeared. Ulysses went back into the hut.

When Telemachus came in through the door, Ulysses was sitting on a stool. Telemachus took one awestruck look at him and fell to his knees.

"Sir, you have changed!" he gasped. "And only the immortal gods can change their appearance. If you are a god, please have mercy on us!"

Ulysses took his son's hands in his. "I am not a god," he said gently, "but I am your father." He looked into his son's frightened, uncomprehending eyes. "I'm sorry, Telemachus," he began. "I'm sorry I've been away all this time, and you've had to grow up without me. Can you forgive me?"

"You're not my father!" shouted Telemachus, standing up. "It must be a trick! No human being, not even Ulysses, can just go changing his appearance whenever he feels like it."

"I am," said Ulysses in exasperation. "That disguise was the work of Athene, who you know is helping us both. I am your father. After nineteen years abroad – and I thought about you every day – here I am."

Telemachus stared at him distrustfully through narrowed eyes. Ulysses couldn't help smiling to see how much Telemachus resembled him – always cunning and thoughtful.

"What? What are you laughing at?" said Telemachus.

"Nothing," said Ulysses. "I was just thinking that we look alike. Don't we?"

"Yes," said Telemachus cautiously.

"Telemachus," Ulysses said at last. "What's your middle name?"

"I never use it," said Telemachus, blushing. Ulysses took his son's arm and drew him closer, whispering a single word in his ear. Aloud, he said, "I gave you that name."

"You are Ulysses," said Telemachus slowly. "Father!" he cried, and burst into tears, flinging his arms around Ulysses. They hugged each other, and then Ulysses stood back to admire again the way his son had grown up so tall, so strong and so like himself. "I do look like you, don't I?" he said.

"But Telemachus," Ulysses continued, sounding more serious, "there's no time for tears. We must do something about those suitors. If we're going to get rid of them, there'll have to be a fight."

"How can we?" said Telemachus despairingly, sitting down heavily on a stool. "I mean, I know you're renowned for your bravery and cunning, and I'd do my best. But there are so many of them, and only two of us."

"Exactly how many?" inquired Ulysses. He looked as if he were thinking up a plan.

"Well..." said Telemachus, "fifty-two from Dulichium, and twenty-four from Same. Another twenty from Zacynthus. And twelve from Ithaca itself. I think. Father, they'd make mincemeat out of you. Even you!"

"But we aren't really alone," Ulysses reminded him. "We do have allies. What about Athene? She is the goddess of wisdom and war. And perhaps she can persuade her father Zeus to help."

Telemachus looked hopelessly miserable.

"Listen," said Ulysses, coming to sit beside him. "Let's try my plan — after all, there's nothing else we can do. This is what I have in mind.

"You'll go down to the palace and take your place there among the suitors. Ignore them if they're horrible to you. Then, I'll come down, disguised as a beggar again, and that way I'll be able to get a good look at them and weigh up our chances.

"When I give you the signal, gather up any of their weapons that are lying around and lock them in the storeroom. If they ask what you're doing, say that you're worried the weapons might get dirty. But remember to leave a couple of things for us to use. And even more importantly, don't tell anyone that I'm back!"

Now Telemachus's ship, which had dropped him off near the farm, sailed into the port of Ithaca's great city. The crew had not been warned to keep quiet, so they ran ashore, crying out to everyone: "A message for the queen! Telemachus is back!"

Eumaeus, who had whispered the message to Penelope herself, realized that the suitors would soon hear the news. He set off back to the farm at once.

It was only a few moments before word got back to the suitors, who were sitting around yet another feast in the palace, that Telemachus had arrived. Eurymachus stood up and banged the table.

"My friends," he announced, "we thought Telemachus had been dealt with. But Antinous's ship must have missed the little squirt. We've got to send a messenger to tell Antinous to come back at once!"

"There he is!" cried Amphinomus, one of the suitors. "No need for a messenger!" He had spied Antinous's ship through the window. It was racing into the port, its sail flapping angrily in the wind. The suitors streamed out of the palace and down to the shore.

"Curse the little fool!" stormed Antinous, as he disembarked a few minutes later. "There we were, waiting around at Asteris, like a bunch of idiots, and Telemachus sails straight past us! He's got some god on his side, I'll bet!"

"So what do we do now, Antinous?" asked Eurymachus, with more than a hint of sarcasm.

"Shut up!" barked Antinous. "If we can't kill him at sea, we'll just have to kill him at home, won't we? When I get my hands on him..."

"But Antinous..." said Amphinomus gingerly, "what if he has got a god on his side? Then we'll be in trouble, if we kill him."

Antinous glared at him.

"I say we consult the oracle," continued Amphinomus. "If we're meant to kill him, the gods will give us a sign!"

"Let's go back inside and have a little more to eat, while we think about it," suggested Eurymachus, and everyone agreed. They wandered back up to the palace.

Penelope was waiting for them.

"Antinous!" she said, biting her lip as if she was trying to control her temper. The suitors shambled around in the doorway while Antinous came guiltily to the front.

"People say, Antinous, that you are wise, that you are charming and clever," she bristled, "but they're wrong! What's this I hear about you going to ambush Telemachus? The gods are to be thanked that you failed! It's bad enough that you all hang around abusing our hospitality and making a nuisance of yourselves. But if you must do that, you could at least leave my son alone!" Her eyes blazed with fury and hatred, directed at Antinous, who, for once, wasn't sure what to say.

"Your Majesty!" It was Eurymachus, using his most charming and polite tone. "How could you think such a thing? It must just be one of the servants gossiping. Why, if anybody hurt Telemachus, they'd soon feel the point of my spear!"

"And mine..." added Antinous, uncertainly.

"We love Telemachus!" Eurymachus went on, getting into his stride. "He's our best friend. Honestly! We all get along like brothers. He has nothing to fear in this house."

Penelope shot him a withering look. Then, holding her head high, she turned on her heels and left the room, her cloak swirling behind her.

But back upstairs, she threw herself on her bed and wept. "I've lost Ulysses," she sobbed, "and now they're going to get Telemachus too. Oh Ulysses, my love! If only you would come home."

The Beggar in the Palace

As Eumaeus toiled up the hill back to his hut, he thought for a moment that there were three people standing outside it. Did he have another visitor?

But as he drew closer he saw that there were only two after all – his master Telemachus, and the old tramp who'd turned up the day before. He didn't see Athene disappearing into the clouds above his head. She'd transformed Ulysses back into a beggar in the nick of time. If Eumaeus had recognized his old master, he'd have been so excited he might have rushed back to the city to tell Penelope, and that would have ruined the goddess's plan.

"Hello, Eumaeus!" said Telemachus, a little nervously. "My... I mean, our, er, old friend here has decided he'd like to try begging at the palace. Could you take him along, later? I'll be leaving myself in a few minutes."

"No, my boy," panted Eumaeus, reaching the top of the slope outside the hut. "You can't go down there – the news is out! All the suitors know you're back, and I'm certain they'll be baying for your blood by now. Telemachus, take an old man's advice and stay up here in the hut, at least until they've calmed down. And as for you, sir," – he turned to Ulysses – "I've told you before, they're not the sort to look kindly on beggars. You stay here as well – goodness knows we've enough pigs to keep you fed!"

"Sorry, Eumaeus," said Telemachus, in a serious voice. "I've got to go. I can't always be hiding away from that crowd of bullies. I've got to face them. When I've been gone for about half an hour, you are to bring our guest to the palace. And that's an order. Goodbye."

Eumaeus looked shocked. "Right you are, sir," he mumbled, as Telemachus picked up his spear and marched off down the hill.

"Well," grumbled Eumaeus, "I can't imagine what's wrong with him." He went on mumbling and shaking his head as he went into the hut and started pottering around.

Ulysses could only smile to himself.

"Telemachus!"

It was one of the maids, busy cleaning the steps of the palace, who first saw Telemachus striding through the gates. She dropped her mop and ran inside. "Telemachus is here!" she shouted to the other women. "Tell my lady the queen it's true, he's back safe and sound!"

Telemachus soon found himself surrounded by maids.

"You've been sorely missed, sir!" cried Eurycleia, his old nurse.

"The suitors have just been getting worse and worse," chimed in Melantho, a young kitchen maid.

"WHERE have you been?"

Penelope had arrived. On her face was an expression of fury mixed with huge relief. "Why did you leave without telling me?" she stormed. Then she threw her arms around her son.

"Oh, Telemachus," she sniffed into his shoulder. "I thought I'd never see you again! The suitors are becoming uncontrollable. What are we to do?"

"Mother, it's all right, I'm safe," Telemachus murmured, hugging her tightly. Since Ulysses had sworn him to secrecy, he thought he'd better not tell her anything.

"Don't worry," he reassured her. "It'll all be over soon. I promise." He hoped he was right.

When his mother had gone back to her room, Telemachus picked up his spear, headed through the hall and out into the grounds. Athene had made him appear even bigger, stronger and better-looking than usual, so that the person the suitors saw pacing up to them over the grass looked like a handsome young god.

Telemachus was expecting snide remarks and mockery from the men who had tried to kill him. But, instead, the suitors seemed to be trying their best to behave.

"Well, Telemachus," said Eurymachus, slapping him on the back. "Pleasant trip? It's good to see you, old friend."

Antinous didn't manage to be quite as polite. "Hello there," he said, trying to twist his sneering face into a welcoming smile.

But Telemachus knew they weren't to be trusted. "I wish I could say it was as pleasant to see you," he said curtly, "but it isn't. There's just one thing I've got to say to you, and you'd better listen..."

"Suppertime!" yelled a maid, and Telemachus was almost crushed by the suitors stampeding to their places around the tables in the hall. Burning with rage and embarrassment, he dusted himself down and followed them in, taking his father's old seat at the top table. He wasn't going to let them get to him.

"You were saying?" Eurymachus asked him sweetly.

"It can wait," said Telemachus, and supper began.

"Who's that?" shouted Antinous an hour later, when the feast was in full swing. There was a commotion in the doorway. Eumaeus, the old swineherd, and Ulysses, disguised as a shabby beggar, were trying to come in, but Argus, Ulysses's old dog, was jumping all over his master and licking his face. "Stupid dog," grumbled Antinous. "Eumaeus, what are you doing here? You've brought today's pork already, haven't you? So get back to the farm!"

"Let them come in," ordered Telemachus loudly. Everyone stared at him. "Eumaeus, come and sit by me. And take this food and give it to our guest." Telemachus filled a plate with meat and bread and handed it to Eumaeus, who trotted back to the doorway with it and handed it to Ulysses.

"Thank you kindly, young sir," Ulysses croaked to Telemachus. He sat down in the doorway to eat.

"Typical," fumed Antinous under his breath.

"And after that, if he's still hungry," said Telemachus as Eumaeus sat down, "tell him to beg a little food from our friends here, the suitors. After all, they're all noblemen," he continued, keeping one eye firmly fixed on Antinous, "and no man of quality turns away a beggar."

Ulysses soon finished his plateful, and realized that he was still hungry. Perhaps Athene had something to do with it, for now he could hear her whispering in his ear, "Go on, do the rounds of the suitors and beg from them. Let's see what they're made of."

So Ulysses got up and hobbled over to the nearest table. He held out his plate and pulled a pathetic, self-pitying face at Leodes, one of the younger suitors.

Leodes wasn't sure what to do. He knew Antinous would shout at him, but Telemachus was right. It was the correct thing to do to take pity on beggars. And what if the beggar was a god in disguise? So he heaped some meat onto Ulysses's plate.

Ulysses trudged along to the next suitor. Under Telemachus's steely glare, Leocritus added a hunk of bread to the plate, giving Antinous an embarrassed shrug. He didn't want to be accused of not being a gentleman.

"This is ridiculous!" yelled Antinous, flinging back his chair and standing up. "You're all under this idiot Telemachus's thumb, aren't you? Eumaeus, why did you bring us this stinking tramp? Don't we have enough people to feed?"

"If we have, it's because you lazy young hooligans are hanging around uninvited all the time," blurted out Eumaeus. "And anyway, I don't have to answer to you, sir. Telemachus is my master, and King Ulysses, if he ever gets home."

By now, Ulysses had trudged around to Antinous's place, and was giving him his most pitiful, long-suffering stare.

"My noble lord," he wheedled, holding out the plate. "Your looks tell me that you're extremely well-bred. Do you have anything to give a poor, weary, unfortunate beggar?"

"A smelly, disgusting, good-for-nothing beggar, more like!" roared Antinous. He grabbed his footstool and lifted it above his head.

"Ah, I can see your brains don't match your looks, after all," said Ulysses with mock sadness, and wandered away from Antinous's table.

This roused Antinous to a raging fury, and he hurled the wooden stool at Ulysses's back. It hit him on the shoulder and bounced onto the floor. Ulysses stopped for a moment, then limped back to the doorway, where he sat down again.

Penelope soon heard from the servants about what Antinous had done. "The bully," she muttered to herself. "They're all rowdy hooligans, but he's by far the worst... Eurycleia!" she called. "Eurycleia!"

The old nurse scurried into the room.

"Eurycleia, I want to meet this beggar who has been so badly treated. Ask him to come and see me."

Eurycleia passed the news to Eumaeus, who went and whispered in Ulysses's ear.

"Tell her I'll see her this evening," said Ulysses. Then, remembering that he was supposed to be a beggar, he added, "Of course, I will gladly meet her majesty. But I'm afraid of these young men – why, when that one over there threw a stool at me, none of the others came to my aid. There's no telling what they'd do to me if they knew I had an audience with the queen. Please tell her I will talk to her after supper." And Eumaeus hurried off.

At that moment, another ragged figure appeared at the doorway. It was Irus, one of Ithaca's regular beggars. He'd been around for years, and often ran errands in exchange for a meal. He was large and stupid, with a very deep voice. "Hey!" he boomed, spying Ulysses. "Who are you? Get off my patch!"

Eurymachus burst out laughing and pointed at the two beggars now facing each other in the doorway. "Nice one, Irus," he snorted. "You tell him!"

"Go on, Irus!" shouted Leocritus. "Kick him out!"

Antinous got up from his place and swaggered over. "Gentlemen!" he announced to the other suitors, "I think we've just found ourselves the perfect after-dinner entertainment. A fight!" The suitors all jumped up, laughing and shouting, and crowded around the beggars, as Irus threw off his dirty cloak and raised his fists. "Come on then!" he taunted.

Ulysses looked at him. Then he calmly pulled up his own ragged sleeves to reveal his bulging muscles. Irus looked shocked. A moment before he'd thought his rival was a weak old man.

"No – wait!" shouted Antinous gleefully. "I've got it! A prize! The winner gets a whole side of pork from the spit. How about it?"

"Er, I think I've changed my mind..." bumbled Irus, but the suitors were having none of it. They pushed him forward, jeering and shouting, "Go on! Hit him, Irus! Give him one from me!"

Ulysses didn't want to kill Irus. So he drew back his fist only half way, and landed a light punch on the beggar's left temple. Irus staggered, fell to his knees with a crunch, and then keeled over into the dust. Ulysses grabbed one of the beggar's arms, dragged him outside, and propped him up against a tree.

"Sorry, Irus," he said. "I think this patch is mine."

The suitors looked pale as they made their way back to their places. Amphinomus quietly went to get the side of pork and presented it to Ulysses. "Well done, sir," he said, avoiding Antinous's gaze. "And good luck to you."

"Thanks, but no thanks," said Ulysses. "It's mine anyway."

Amphinomus looked puzzled. "Listen, Amphinomus," said Ulysses quietly. "I knew your father once, Nisus of Dulichium. He was a good man, and I think you are too, at heart. So I'm going to be frank with you."

Amphinomus stared at him, wide-eyed.

"The gods don't look kindly on men who abuse others' hospitality, overstay their welcome and plot to murder their host."

Amphinomus's eyes nearly popped out of his head. He wondered if the beggar really was a god in disguise.

"And I can tell you for certain that it won't be long before Ulysses is back. In fact," he said, leaning forward and staring into Amphinomus's face, "he's very close indeed. So watch out."

"What's going on?" shouted Eurymachus. "Now that you've won a fight, you think you're the greatest, don't you? Well shut up, and go and sit back down in the doorway where you belong!" Then he too picked up his stool, and threw it in Ulysses's direction. It missed, and hit Leodes. He yelled, grabbed the stool and flung it back. Suddenly the whole hall was in uproar, with the suitors shouting and hurling food, furniture and plates at each other.

"Stop this at once!" bellowed Telemachus above the din. His voice was so loud that it cut through the noise and stopped the suitors in their tracks. They looked at him, astonished.

"I've had enough of this!" Telemachus roared, his eyes darting wildly from one suitor to another. "You can all go and stay with your friends in Ithaca tonight. Get out of my palace. GET OUT!"

The suitors were so surprised that they dropped the things they were holding and started wandering sheepishly over to the door. Only Antinous tried to answer back.

"Who do you think you are?" he barked at Telemachus. "Hey! All of you! Don't take orders from him!" But the hall was emptying. Furiously, Antinous followed the crowd. As he left, he turned around and said, "Well, don't think we're going for good. We'll be back tomorrow. And we'll stay until your mother makes a decision." With that, he stomped off.

"Well done." Ulysses squeezed Telemachus's trembling shoulder.

"It's no use though," sighed Telemachus. "They'll be back first thing in the morning."

"Good," said Ulysses. "I'd hate it if they got away with it, after all they've put you through. But for now, you've created the ideal opportunity for us to hide those weapons." He scanned the hall. Tables were overturned, food was splattered across the white marble walls. "We'll get the servants to clean up, while we take all those weapons they've left lying around, and lock them in that storeroom."

The weapons were all locked away, except for a few which Telemachus had hidden in a wooden chest by the doorway. Telemachus had gone to bed, and Ulysses was sitting in the hall in darkness when Penelope and the nurse, Eurycleia, came down.

"Where is everybody?" asked the queen.

"All gone, my lady," said Ulysses through the darkness. "The young master has sent them packing. But I'm here to see you, as you requested."

Eurycleia lit a lamp and Ulysses's old, wrinkled face flickered into view.

"Old man," said Penelope gently, sitting down opposite him. To Ulysses, she looked every bit as beautiful as she had on the day he'd left for Troy, nineteen years before. But he was unable to touch her, or to tell her who he was.

"First of all, I must apologize for the rudeness of some of our guests here," Penelope said. "I must take responsibility, as they are my suitors. But I wish they were gone," she added, looking angrily away. "I wish my beloved husband would come home and reclaim his throne." Regaining her composure, she carried on, "And that's what I wanted to ask you about. You move around a lot. Have you ever... did you by any chance hear anything? About him? Ulysses, that is?"

"Well..." began Ulysses, his brain racing. "Yes... yes, I did."

Penelope stepped forward out of her chair and took Ulysses's wrinkled hands in hers. "Please, please tell me anything you know," she begged. "You may name your reward."

"No reward, my lady," Ulysses replied. "I'll tell you all I can. I knew Ulysses at Troy. And there he fought like a demon, like a mighty whirlwind. And his cunning was second to none. Why, he almost won the Trojan War on his own."

"And... did he escape?" asked Penelope.

"Oh, yes. But he was doomed to wander the world, chased by murderous monsters, trapped by wicked witches, pounded by perilous sea storms – until he came to the land of Phaeacia."

"Phaeacia! But's that's not far from here at all," gasped Penelope. Then her eyes narrowed. "How do you know all this?" she asked.

"Oh, I visited Phaeacia recently," said Ulysses hurriedly. "Anyway, word has it that he's coming back very soon."

Penelope's hand went up to her mouth. "Really?" she asked, softly.

"Yes," said Ulysses, almost in a whisper. "In fact, he's very close."

"Oh!" Penelope looked troubled. "But... how do I know you're talking about the real Ulysses? You might have mixed him up with someone else. Describe him for me."

"Well," said Ulysses, "he's tall, and handsome, and very muscular. And when I saw him, he had this brooch – pure gold, with an image of a hound catching a deer. Beautiful, it was."

"That's him!" cried Penelope. "I gave him that brooch when he left for Troy." She stood up and started pacing the room. "But I can't believe he's really coming home. It's been so long! Old man, what do you think I should do? Should I wait for him? Or should I choose one of the suitors, just to get the rest of them to leave? I had such a strange dream..." she went on, without giving him time to answer. "I dreamed that a huge eagle flew down and killed all the fat white geese in the courtyard. What do you think that means?" She turned to face Ulysses, her face a mask of fear and uncertainty.

"It means, my lady," Ulysses said patiently, "that Ulysses will descend on this house, and kill those suitors who have been making free with his property and harassing his wife, as well as threatening his son."

But Penelope ignored him. She was obviously thinking about something completely different.

"I know what I'll do," she announced decisively. "I've been planning it for a while, in fact. My husband used to be a great archer, and his bow is still in one of the palace storerooms. He was the only person in Ithaca strong enough to string it. For practice, he used to shoot a bronze-tipped arrow through the handles of twelve axes, all stuck in the ground in a row.

"I'm going to hold a competition," she declared. "I'm going to get that old bow out, and let the suitors try to shoot through the axes, as my husband used to. If any one of them can do it, well, I'll think about marrying him."

Little did Penelope realize that Athene had put the plan into her head.

"You must do as your heart commands, my lady," said Ulysses, smiling to himself.

Penelope turned to him. "Thank you, sir, for your wise words," she said. But she seemed distracted. She was thinking about the competition. It was a good plan, but what if one of the suitors did succeed?

"I'm going to bed now," she said. "I'll have a mattress put down for you here in the hall. The servants will bring you some blankets." Her voice echoed behind her as she disappeared into the darkness of the hall.

The Final Challenge

Ulysses woke with the dawn. No one was about in the hall. He went outside, feeling the cold, dewy grass beneath his bare feet, and looked up at the pink-tinged sky.

"Father Zeus," he whispered. "Please, send me a sign. If today is the day when I will battle with the suitors – send me a sign."

A rumbling sound began in the far north. It grew and grew until a huge roaring noise echoed around the whole sky, and culminated in a thunderous crash right above the palace. Then, all was silent.

Ulysses hugged himself, hopping from one foot to another and clenching his fists in excitement. "Yes!" he whispered. "Yes. Today's the day."

Telemachus had been right that the suitors wouldn't be away for long. By the time he'd dressed and come downstairs, there they all were, lying around in the palace grounds, drinking.

But Amphinomus wasn't happy. He was thinking about the mysterious warning the old beggar had given him the day before. What had he said about Ulysses? He's very close indeed – that was it.

Amphinomus plucked up his courage and strode over to Antinous.

"Hello," he said. "Just came by to talk." He sat down next to Antinous and started twiddling his thumbs.

"What do you want, Amphinomus?" snapped Antinous. "Spit it out."

"Well, it's about killing Telemachus," Amphinomus stuttered. "I mean, er, perhaps we shouldn't..."

"Oh, I see," mocked Antinous loudly, so that several other suitors looked round. "Chicken, are we? Chicken, Amphinomus?" Antinous stood up and started flapping his elbows and squawking. "Oh, count me out," he squealed. "I'm chicken!"

"No, you don't understand" said Amphinomus hurriedly. "You see, the thing is, that old beggar..."

"Yes, that disgusting old cripple," snarled Antinous, "I'd forgotten about him."

"I vote we kill them both," said Eurymachus.

"Excellent idea!" said Antinous. He turned to the crowd of suitors that had gathered around him, and said, "Listen, I've got a plan. All we need to do is make sure Penelope's out of the way, surround Telemachus in the hall, and..."

"Look!" shrieked Amphinomus, pointing above their heads.

The suitors all looked up in the air. There, only feet above them, a huge, black eagle was grappling with a terrified pigeon. The suitors could feel the wind from the eagle's huge, beating wings as it tore viciously at the pigeon's neck with its talons. Feathers swirled down, several of them landing on Antinous's head. Then the eagle swerved off to the left and flapped away, the dead pigeon hanging limply in its claws.

"Antinous!" gasped Amphinomus, hardly able to speak for trembling.

"Y-you know what that was... An omen! That eagle must have stood for Ulysses, and that pigeon... Antinous, that was you."

"Shut up, you soppy idiot!" Antinous raged. "We can do without your pathetic, stupid omens. It was an eagle, that's all! And if you open your mouth one more time, Amphinomus, I'll..."

"Hello, boys!"

Penelope had appeared on the palace steps. Flanked by maids, she stood erect, tall and beautiful, her silver-embroidered gown gleaming in the sun. The suitors quickly turned around and smiled broadly at the queen. Each of them wanted Penelope to like him best.

"You'll be pleased to hear," Penelope announced, "that I've decided to hold a competition, to see who will be my husband. I'd like you all to assemble in the courtyard." And with that, she and her maids glided back inside.

"See," mocked Antinous as they all filed through the hall into the courtyard. "Ulysses is dead – he must be, or she wouldn't be doing this, would she?"

Penelope unlocked the storeroom using her set of keys, and stepped into the gloom. There seemed to be

a lot more weapons in here than she remembered, but she soon found what she was looking for – her husband's great bow. It was hanging on the wall, covered in a thick layer of dust. She took it down carefully. It was heavy, and almost as tall as she was.

For a moment, Penelope stood in the dank, sunless storeroom, clutching the bow.

"Madam?" called a maid from outside. "Are you all right?"

"Yes," said Penelope quickly. "Yes, I am." She started picking out old axes and handing them back to the servants at the door. Then they set off for the courtyard. The door to the storeroom banged shut, but she didn't lock it.

"Now," said Penelope, as cheerily as possible, as the maids piled up the axes on the grass. "This bow belonged to my dear husband. He used to be able to shoot an arrow through the handles of twelve axes, all in a row. So, gentlemen, I challenge you to do the same. If any one of you can prove yourselves as strong and clever as my husband... well." Penelope couldn't quite bring herself to say it. "We'll see," she said, finally, then went and sat on a throne brought outside by her servants.

Standing at the edge of the crowd, Telemachus glanced at his father nervously. "Is this all right?" he said in an urgent whisper. "I mean, what if one of them does it?"

"They won't," said Ulysses. "Athene's behind this. Keep a straight face, and wait for my instructions."

The suitors set to work ramming the axe handles into the ground. Then they started arguing over who should go first.

"Youngest first!" shouted Leocritus. "No, let's do it in alphabetical order!" yelled a suitor named Agelaus.

"What about the order we sit in for dinner?" asked Amphinomus. No one could think of a better idea, so Leodes was first to try.

Trying to look like an experienced archer, Leodes strolled over to the bow and picked it up. The first job was to string it, as the bowstring was hanging loose. Leodes tried to grip the huge bow between his knees while he reached up to loop the string over the other end. But it was just too short. To tie it on, Leodes had to bend the bow, but however hard he tried, he couldn't keep it bent and tie the string at the same time.

The suitors slapped their thighs and roared with laughter as Leodes grappled hopelessly with the bow. Eventually, after it had sprung out of his hands and hit him on the nose, he flung the bow on the grass and stormed, red-faced with embarassment, back into the crowd.

"Who's next?" called Telemachus, trying not to look smug. Leocritus came forward. He was even younger and slighter than Leodes, and he was having an equally hard time with the bow, when Telemachus saw Eumaeus, the swineherd, approaching the palace gates. With him was Philoetius, who looked after the cows. Each of them was leading several animals, ready for the evening meal.

Telemachus slipped out of the courtyard to greet them. Ulysses hobbled after him.

"You'd better tie the animals up around the back," said Telemachus. "They're having an archery competition in there. Whoever wins might be getting married soon."

"What, my lady's going to pick one of those young good-for-nothings?" gasped Eumaeus.

"Eumaeus," Ulysses interrupted. "And you, sir, what's your name?"

"Philoetius," answered the young cowherd.

Ulysses glanced at Telemachus, then beckoned all three men over. "I want to ask you something. If Ulysses arrived right now to fight those suitors – what would you do? Would you be on his side? Would you fight for him?"

"I would, sir," said Philoetius. "Though he left before I was born, and folk say he'll never be seen around these parts again, I know he's our rightful leader, sir."

"Of course I would, what do you take me for?" grumbled Eumaeus. "But he's not coming back, is he? We've waited and waited. I dare say he's been dead for years."

"That's where you're wrong," said Ulysses. "Here I am. It's me. Ulysses."

"What?" said Philoetius.

"No, it's not," said Eumaeus. "You're not Ulysses. You're an old man, he'd be, what... how old was he when you were born, Telemachus?"

"This is my father!" Telemachus told the two farmers. "He is back. But he's in disguise. Athene disguised him as a beggar."

"Why?" said Philoetius.

"Nonsense," snorted Eumaeus, "he's pulling your leg!"

"I am Ulysses," said Ulysses through gritted teeth. "Prove it, then," said Philoetius boldly.

Ulysses pulled up the rags covering his legs, and showed his right thigh to Eumaeus. "Look," he said. "I got this scar chasing wild boars at my grandfather's house, didn't I?"

In disbelief, Eumaeus dropped his rope tether. The pigs started to wander off.

"And I know all about you, Eumaeus. My father Laertes rescued you when you were a little boy, from a trading ship that had kidnapped you from Syrie, didn't he?"

"Ulysses," said Eumaeus in a barely audible whisper, his eyes filling with tears. He gripped Philoetius's arm. "It is him! It is him! Oh, my lord and master, the gods be praised!" And he threw his arms around Ulysses's neck.

"There's no time to lose," said Ulysses, when Eumaeus had stopped weeping. "I intend to make my move while the competition is going on. Are you really prepared to fight with me?"

"I'd give my life!" wailed Eumaeus.

"No need for that," said Ulysses kindly, "as Athene is on our side. If you follow my instructions, I'm confident of our success. Philoetius, you are to bolt all the doors, locking us inside. Tie the main gates shut with a rope, then come and join us in the courtyard.

"Eumaeus, your job is to get the maidservants out of the way. They must all be locked safely in their quarters. Then come to the courtyard. When you hear me ask if I can have a try with the bow, don't wait. Go and get it and hand it to me, whatever the suitors say.

"And Telemachus," said Ulysses finally, turning to his son, "your job is to make sure your mother is out of the way too. She must be safe in her room before the battle can begin. Then, when I give the signal, I want you to leap up onto the steps leading from the courtyard into the hall. From there we'll begin our attack.

"And none of you must breathe a word to anyone that I'm here."

While the other two raced off to carry out their instructions, Ulysses and Telemachus strolled back to the courtyard. The suitors were sitting around looking disgruntled, while Eurymachus struggled with the bow. Behind him sat Penelope, with a satisfied smile on her face.

"Oh, there you are, Telemachus!" taunted Antinous. "Still hanging around with that beggar?"

"Hello, Antinous," replied Telemachus calmly. "How's it going?"

"Ow!" shouted Eurymachus as the bow sprang from his grasp and smacked him in the forehead. "It's useless! Everyone's given it a try, but no one can even string it! It's embarrassing, that's what it is. What will people say when they hear what weaklings we are compared to Ulysses? We'll never live it down!"

"Excuse me," began Ulysses, stepping forward. "But could I try?"

"You?" gaped Antinous incredulously. "You? You don't think Penelope's going to marry you, do you?"

"No," said Ulysses, "I don't think that will be necessary. I just wanted to try my hand at it, that's all."

"Go on, let him try," said Eurymachus, who was bored with trying.

"No way!" Antinous stood up. "Why doesn't that stupid tramp stop bothering us, anyway?" But underneath his rude exterior, Antinous was thinking about how easily the beggar had knocked out Irus in the fight. What if he was strong enough to handle the bow? The suitors would never hear the end of it.

"Antinous!" boomed Penelope. "I'm in charge here. Let the old man try. Of course I'm not going to marry him. If he meets the challenge, I'll give him a new set of clothes."

"No, I'm in charge here!" said Telemachus, striding over to Penelope. "And I suggest, Mother, that you go to your room before this gets out of hand."

Penelope looked aghast at her son for speaking to her so rudely. Telemachus stepped nearer to her.

"Go on," he said under his breath. "I'm sorry. I'll explain later."

Grabbing handfuls of her skirt, Penelope rose elegantly from her throne and swept across the courtyard, followed by a gaggle of maids. She disappeared through the door that led to her room.

No one noticed Philoetius bolting it tightly as he sidled past.

Meanwhile, Eumaeus had picked up the bow and arrows. On either side, suitors jeered and spat at him as he plodded up the courtyard and carefully handed the weapons over to his master.

In a couple of seconds, Ulysses had expertly strung his old bow and was flexing it back and forth. The suitors stared, open-mouthed.

"Stand back," croaked Ulysses. "Let me get a good shot."

Unwillingly, the suitors shuffled back a few steps.

Ulysses selected an arrow. Its bronze tip gleamed in the sunlight as he laid it against the bow, drew back the bowstring, and took aim.

There was silence. Then there was a twang and a whistle of air

143

as the arrow left the bow, and a series of satisfying splintering noises as it sliced right through the middle of the handle of every single axe in the row.

Antinous went pale. Some of the suitors were about to cheer the beggar's effort when they noticed that he was swiftly reloading the bow with another deadly, bronze-tipped arrow. As he did so, Ulysses glanced meaningfully at Telemachus, Eumaeus and the cowherd, Philoetius, who followed him onto the marble steps.

"What's going on?" shrieked Antinous desperately.

"Oh no!" wailed Amphinomus.

THWACK! Ulysses's second arrow had hit its target.

Antinous lay sprawling and writhing on the grass, his legs kicking violently. The arrow had torn right through his neck, pinning him to the ground. Blood spurted from the wound and soaked the grass around his head.

"Aaaaeeeurggghhh!" groaned Antinous. He wriggled, helplessly, one last time. Then his body lay still.

A sea of pale, terrified faces now surrounded the four men on the steps.

"L-look what you've done now," said Eurymachus, trembling. "You'd better put the bow down. That was a foolish mistake."

"It wasn't a mistake," said Ulysses. And at that moment, Athene made his rags fall away and replaced

them with a tunic and a gleaming breastplate. She made his hair thicker and changed it from wispy white back to glossy black. She pumped up his muscles, smoothed away his wrinkles, and made him taller than ever.

"I'M BACK!" roared Ulysses.

Frantically, the suitors began hunting around for any weapons they could find. But there were none in the courtyard, and the door into the hall was blocked by Ulysses. Starting to panic, they backed up against the locked gates, each one trying to hide behind the others.

"Don't just stand there cowering and waiting to be killed," shouted Eurymachus. "He's going to shoot us all unless we do something. I say we fight!" He drew a small dagger, the only weapon he was carrying, and rushed at Ulysses.

WHOOSH! The third arrow shot through the air and thudded into Eurymachus's chest. He gulped and staggered back, and the silver dagger fell, uselessly, from his slackening hand. Finally, he crashed into the row of splintered axes and crumpled into a heap.

"Telemachus," whispered Ulysses, "bring the weapons from the store-room."

Telemachus tiptoed away as the suitors, following Eurymachus's example, began to edge forward, clutching their daggers. While he rummaged desperately in the storeroom where the weapons were hidden, Telemachus heard more arrows swishing through the air, more screams and more thuds. When he hurried back, carrying helmets, spears and shields, he could see many more bodies scattered across the grass.

"Quick! I'm nearly out of arrows," panted Ulysses as he grabbed a spear. Eumaeus and Philoetius, who had been standing on the steps wide-eyed with panic, fumbled as they tied on their helmets and each took a spear and a shield.

"What's going on? Father, look!" shouted

Telemachus as six suitors advanced on them, each carrying a long, silver-tipped spear. "Where did they get those from?"

"The storeroom, of course," yelled Leodes. "Very sneaky of you to hide away our weapons. But you forgot to lock the door!"

At that moment the suitors flung their weapons, and the shower of spears hurtled through the air. But Athene had not deserted Ulysses. She redirected the spears away from their targets, and they clattered against the marble walls of the courtyard. "Give them the same back," Athene whispered.

The four men drew back their spears and hurled them as one into the crowd. Athene directed each spear into the heart of a suitor. The other suitors retreated in panic, and Ulysses and his comrades rushed forward to retrieve their weapons.

"Again," whispered Athene. Ulysses felt a new surge of energy suffuse his body as he drew back his spear a second time. And again, Athene sent all four weapons whistling through the air to their targets, but in the same instant, six more spears came speeding back at them. This time, one of the suitors' weapons sliced through the flesh of Telemachus's right arm. But taking his spear again in his left hand, he hurled it with all his strength along with the others, and four more suitors fell to the ground.

"I beg you, save me!" One of the few men left alive in the courtyard hurried up to the steps. "It's me, Medon, the herald. I was your loyal servant, sir, but the suitors forced me to serve them. Please..."

"You served my enemies!" roared Ulysses, dizzy with bloodlust and adrenalin. Grabbing Medon by the hair, he pulled out his dagger.

"Father! No!" Telemachus wrestled with Ulysses's arm. "He's innocent! Spare him – and poor Phemius, our minstrel, who was forced to play for them." Phemius, hearing his name, crawled out from behind a pile of bodies, soaked in blood. Telemachus took both men by the arm and led them into the safety of the hall.

When Telemachus came back out, clutching his bleeding arm, there was silence. Ulysses was leaning on the steps, breathlessly wiping his face with his sweaty arm. Eumaeus was standing and staring into space, shellshocked, his blood-stained spear dangling loosely in his grasp. Philoetius sat a little way off, his face in his hands. The whole courtyard was filled with dead bodies, spreadeagled on the grass, sprawled against the walls and lying broken on the steps. The sickening stench of blood filled the air.

Telemachus approached his father and tried to touch his shoulder. Ulysses looked away from him and sat down heavily on the step. "Find my wife," he mumbled.

Telemachus unbolted the door and sprinted up the steps to Penelope's chambers. As he threw open the door, Penelope and her maids screamed.

Penelope stood up and came over to him, her face a terrified mask. She touched the blood on his arm. "What's been going on, Telemachus?"

"My father is home," said Telemachus, wiping his lip. "There's... well, there's been a battle. I think you should come downstairs and see him."

When the crowd of women filed out of the doorway into the bright sunlight of the courtyard, they gasped in horror at the terrible sight. Then, seeing Ulysses, they began to shout and cheer, and eagerly surrounded him, asking him questions and trying to touch him. Only Penelope stood alone on the other side of the courtyard, staring quietly at the man in the middle of the crowd.

"This isn't a time for celebration," said Ulysses at last. His voice was stern. "These men fell victims to the hands of the gods, and must be buried. Carry out the bodies and clean up the courtyard." The servants drew back from him in awe, and turned to their gruesome work.

Ulysses stared at Penelope. She stared back. Neither of them spoke.

"Mother..." began Telemachus. "Aren't you going to greet my father?"

"Telemachus," she said painfully, holding out her hand to her son. "My heart has gone numb. I don't know what to say to him."

"It is your husband," said Telemachus kindly. "Don't you want to be alone with him?" Ulysses stared at them anxiously.

"If it is him," said Penelope, swallowing hard, "then he'll survive a night alone outside my bedroom, as a test of his love. Tell Eurycleia to move my bed out of the room for him."

"No!" roared Ulysses suddenly. "How can that bed be moved? I built that bedroom myself around a tall olive tree, and made its trunk into one of the bedposts!"

"Ulysses..." said Penelope faintly. Now she knew it was him. Her eyes filled with tears. "My husband..." Her legs gave way and she crumpled onto the steps as Ulysses bounded forward and threw his arms around her. "My love," he whispered.

The servants and Telemachus crept away into the hall, leaving Ulysses and Penelope alone.

"This way!" called Hermes, messenger of the gods, clutching his golden wand. Groaning and wailing, weeping and moaning, the ghosts of the suitors floated after him, past the River of Ocean, through the region of dreams, and down into the depths of Hades, the dwelling-place of the dead.

"Who's there?" barked Persephone, Queen of the Underworld, as they approached. "It is Antinous," groaned the soul of Antinous as it fluttered in through the gates, its face already green with decay, "and my comrades, victims of the brave warrior Ulysses, who has killed us all. Oh, if only I'd listened to Amphinomus..."

"He's done it! Ulysses has done it!" The soul of

Agamemnon clenched its fists jubilantly. "Well done, Ulysses! I knew he'd come up with the goods. Tell us what happened, then."

And so the ghosts of Antinous and the others told the dead how Ulysses had returned as a beggar to his own palace, how he had tried to warn the suitors, and how he had fought with Athene's help in the battle that had ended their lives. The soul of Agamemnon twirled around with delight. "He's lost none of his cunning," it grinned.

"But our families will avenge us," wailed Antinous's soul. "And Ulysses himself will be down here with us before you know it!"

Outside the royal palace in Ithaca, the families of the dead were gathering. "Come out and show yourself, murderer!" they yelled. "Ulysses, you coward! Come out and fight!"

Suddenly, the sky was filled with a bright pink glow. A figure appeared before them, descending slowly, eyes flashing, a long, shining spear in her grasp. The families shrank back, shading their eyes and gawping in amazement.

"People of Ithaca, Same, Dulichium and Zacynthus!" Athene boomed, her voice echoing around the city. "Justice, not murder, has been done in this city."

The families gaped at the goddess in awe. Behind them, the people of Ithaca were streaming out of their houses and crowding around the palace, gazing at the incredible sight of the goddess hovering in midair in front of the palace.

"There is only one rightful ruler of Ithaca," she cried, "and he is no coward! He has done battle with monsters and murderers, witches and whirlpools, giants and the looming shadow of death itself, and he has survived to fight the insolent wretches who would have stolen his wife and destroyed his kingdom. Are these the fools you came to defend? They deserved to die; the gods ordained it. Do you wish to fight the murderer?"

She glowed more brightly and terrifyingly than ever. "I am the murderer!" she roared. "Are you going to fight me?"

There was silence. Everyone hoped someone else would dare to speak to the goddess of wisdom and war. But no one did.

"Good," boomed Athene. "Then I suggest you bow down before your king, Ulysses, who has returned after nineteen years, to rule this land as wisely and as well as any god."

And with that, she shot up into the clouds like a firework.

When Ulysses and Penelope came out of the courtyard gates to find out what was happening, they saw hundreds of people, the people of their country, kneeling before them on the soft, grassy slope that led down from the palace. Penelope came to the front of the steps, leading her husband by the hand.

"Citizens of Ithaca!" she cried out. "Rise up and greet your king!"

Gradually, falteringly, the people began to stand. The bright light that had accompanied Athene was gone, replaced by normal sunshine. The people took their hands away from their eyes.

Ulysses stepped forward and cleared his throat.

"I have an apology to make," he began. A murmur of surprise spread through the crowd. People strained forward to hear what he had to say.

"Those young men didn't deserve such a terrible end. I did try to warn them – but they were stubborn. I am sorry that some of you have lost your sons and brothers. They brought their fate on themselves, but their punishment was far worse than was fitting. It was an act of the gods – and that means we must give them a proper burial."

Some of the suitors' relations were weeping quietly. Others hung their heads. Nisus of Dulichium, the father of Amphinomus, came forward.

"Friends, we must accept this apology," he said. "Retaliation won't get us anywhere. Athene was right. We must respect our rightful king." The families of the suitors nodded sadly.

"Now I am home," continued Ulysses. "I hope we Ithacans can stand together, and put all these horrors behind us. The Trojan War is won. Your rightful king has returned. Peace and prosperity will rule again in Ithaca!"

Now the people let out a huge cheer. "But," shouted Ulysses, raising his hand to quieten them, "if ever I have to leave Ithaca again, while I'm away, power will rest with my wife, Penelope, and my son, Telemachus – your future king."

At that moment, Telemachus stepped out of the courtyard gates, blinking in the sunshine. An even bigger roar went up, and the people surged forward and lifted him off his feet, shouting his name, waving and cheering. And in this way, the whole population of the city swarmed down the hill and onto the shore.

There, they knelt to give thanks to the gods. And when the suitors had been buried, they held a huge feast and made sacrifices to the gods – to Zeus, Hermes, Helios and even to Poseidon, and most of all to beautiful Athene, whose wisdom and guidance had brought their leader safely home.

Who's Who and Important Places

Achilles (a-*kill*-ees) Greek soldier, a hero of the Trojan War.

Aegisthus (ee-*gis*-thus) Lover of Agamemnon's wife Clytemnestra, and murderer of Agamemnon.

Aeolus (ee-*ole*-us) King of Aeolia and ruler of the winds.

Agamemnon (ag-a-*mem*-non) Brother of Menelaus and one of the Greeks who fought in the Trojan War. He was murdered by his wife, Clytemnestra, and her lover, Aegisthus, when he returned. Ulysses meets him in the Land of the Dead.

Agelaus (a-ge-*lay*-us) One of Penelope's suitors.

Alcinous (al-*sin*-o-us) King of Phaeacia who helps Ulysses to return home to Ithaca.

Amphinomus (am-*fin*-o-mus) One of Penelope's suitors.

Anticleia (an-ti-*clay*-a) Ulysses's mother. She died of grief while Ulysses was away. Ulysses meets her in the Land of the Dead.

Antinous (an-*tin*-o-us) Leader of Penelope's suitors.

Arete (a-*ret*-ee) Queen of Phaeacia, wife of Alcinous and mother of Nausicaa.

Argus (*are*-gus) Ulysses's dog.

Athene (a-*thee*-nee) Goddess of wisdom and war, daughter of Zeus and step-daughter of Hera.

Calypso (ka-*lip*-so) Nymph who holds Ulysses prisoner.

Charybdis (ka-*rib*-dis) A deadly whirlpool.

Circe (*sir*-see) Minor goddess and powerful sorceress who turns some of Ulysses's men into pigs and then entraps him for a year.

Clytemnestra (*kly*-tum-nes-tra) Wife of Agamemnon, whom she plots to kill when he returns from the Trojan War.

Cyclops (*sye*-klops) (plural: Cyclopes – *sye*-klo-peas) A one-eyed giant. Ulysses enrages the sea god Poseidon by blinding Poseidon's son, the Cyclops Polyphemus.

Demodocus (de-*mod*-o-kus) Bard (singing poet) at the court of King Alcinous in Phaeacia.

Echeneus (e-ke-*nay*-us) Lord at Alcinous's court in Phaeacia.

Eidothee (ay-*doh*-thee) Daughter of Proteus, the Old Man of the Sea.

Elpenor (*el*-pen-or) Young member of Ulysses's crew who dies after falling off the roof of Circe's cottage.

Eugenie (yoo-*gee*-nee) Friend of Nausicaa, the Phaeacian princess.

Eumaeus (yoo-*may*-us) Ulysses's faithful swineherd in Ithaca.

Eurycleia (yoo-ri-*clay*-a) Penelope's chief lady-in-waiting.

Eurylochus (yoo-*ril*-o-kus) Ulysses's most senior crew member.

Eurymachus (yoo-*rim*-a-kus) One of Penelope's suitors.

Helen (*hell*-en) Wife of Menelaus.

Helios (*hee*-lee-oss) God of the sun.

Hermes (*her*-mees) Messenger of the gods and son of Zeus. He leads dying people down into the Underworld.

Ino (*ee*-no) A minor sea goddess.

Irus (*eye*-rus) An Ithacan beggar.

Laertes (lay-*er*-tees) Ulysses's father, husband of Anticleia.

Leocritus (lay-*o*-crit-us) One of Penelope's suitors.

Leodes (lay-*oh*-dees) One of Penelope's suitors.

Lotus-eaters (*low*-tuss eaters) People who live on the fruit of the lotus plant, which makes them forget everything except wanting to eat more of the fruit.

Medon (*med*-on) Herald (servant who makes announcements) at Ulysses's palace.

Melantho (me-*lan*-tho) Maid at Ulysses's palace in Ithaca.

Menelaus (me-ne-*lay*-us) King of Sparta, brother of Agamemnon, husband of Helen, a Greeks hero of the Trojan War.

Mentes (*men*-tees) Name assumed by Athene when she first visits Telemachus.

Mentor (*men*-tor) A friend of Ulysses, and the name assumed by Athene when she goes with Telemachus to look for Ulysses.

Nausicaa (nor-*zik*-ay-a) Princess of Phaeacia, daughter of King Alcinous and Queen Arete. She finds Ulysses washed up on the shores of Phaeacia and invites him back to the palace.

Nestor (*nes*-tor) King of Pylos, and one of the Greeks who fought with Ulysses in the Trojan War.

Nisus (*nee*-sus) Father of Penelope's suitor Amphinomus.

Noemon (no-*ay*-mon) Ithacan who lends Telemachus a ship.

Nymphs (*nimphs*) Demigoddesses (half god, half human); spirits of water, trees and mountains.

Odysseus (o-*dee*-si-us) Another name for Ulysses.

Peisistratus (pie-*siss*-tra-tus) Son of King Nestor. He accompanies Telemachus to Sparta on his search for Ulysses.

Penelope (pe-*nell*-o-pee) Queen of Ithaca, Ulysses's wife and mother of Telemachus. When her husband does not return from the Trojan War, she is beseiged by admirers who want to marry her to gain possession of the royal palace.

Persephone (per-*seff*-o-nee) Goddess of death and guardian of the Land of the Dead.

Phemius (*fee*-mi-us) Bard (singing poet) at Ulysses's palace.

Philoetius (fill-oh-*ee*-shus) Ithacan cowherd.

Polites (po-*lee*-tees) Member of Ulysses's crew.

Polyphemus (polly-*fee*-muss) The Cyclops that Ulysses meets and tricks. Son of Poseidon.

Poseidon (poss-*eye*-don) Bad-tempered god of the Sea, brother of Zeus and father of Polyphemus, the Cyclops.

Proteus (*proh*-ti-us) The Old Man of the Sea, a minor sea god.

Scylla (*sill*-a) A man-eating monster with six heads.

Sirens (*sye*-runs) Monsters with the faces of beautiful women. They live on a rocky island and lure men to their doom with their singing.

Teiresias (ty-*ree*-zi-as) A soothsayer (fortune-teller) whom Ulysses meets in the Land of the Dead.

Telemachus (te-*lem*-a-kus) The son of Ulysses and Penelope, grandson of Laertes and Anticleia, and future King of Ithaca. He is only a baby when his father leaves for the Trojan War.

Ulysses (*yoo*-liss-ees) King of Ithaca, son of Laertes and Anticleia, husband of Penelope, father of Telemachus. Greek hero of the Trojan War, known for his cleverness and cunning. Because he displeases the gods, it takes him nineteen years to get home from the war. Also known as Odysseus (o-*dee*-si-us).

Zeus (*zyoos*) King of the gods and father of the human race. Ruler of the sky. Married to his sister, Hera. Rules from Mount Olympus and often gets involved in human affairs. All-powerful.

Important Places

Aeolia Island, home of King Aeolus, ruler of the winds.

Asteris Island where Penelope's suitors wait to ambush Telemachus.

Cythera Island that Ulysses passes when he is blown off course.

Dulichium Land near Ithaca, home of some of Penelope's suitors.

Hades *See* Land of the Dead.

Ithaca Island, Ulysses's home.

Land of the Dead Underground kingdom to which the Ancient Greeks believed all humans went when they died. Also called Hades, and the Underworld.

Mount Neriton Mountain and main landmark on Ithaca.

Mount Olympus The mountain where the Ancient Greeks believed Zeus and other gods and goddesses live.

Ogygia Calypso's island.

Phaeacia Island kingdom, ruled by King Alcinous and Queen Arete, where Ulysses tells stories of his adventures.

Pharos Egyptian island where Menelaus met Proteus and found out about Ulysses.

Pylos Home of King Nestor, visited by Telemachus on his search for Ulysses.

River of Ocean River by which dying people were believed to reach the Land of the Dead.

Same Land near Ithaca, home of some of Penelope's suitors.

Solymi Mountains Mountains where Poseidon rests on his way home from Africa.

Sparta Home of Menelaus, visited by Telemachus on his search for Ulysses.

Taphos Land Athene names as her home when she first appears (as "Mentes") to Telemachus.

Troy City where the Greeks fought a ten-year war to retrieve Helen, who had been abducted by Paris, Prince of Troy.

Underworld *See* Land of the Dead.

Zacynthus Land near Ithaca, home of some of Penelope's suitors.